The Memory Editor

By

Donna H. Black

Passiflora
PUBLISHING

The Memory Editor

Published by Passiflora Publishing, Fayetteville, GA

Cover Photograph: iStock.com/Vitalij Sova

Cover Design: Donna Black

For information and permission to reproduce any portion
of this book, contact the author at:
donnablackwrites@gmail.com

LIBRARY OF CONGRESS CATALOGING-IN-
PUBLICATION DATA

Black, Donna H., 2020

The Memory Editor: a novella / Donna H. Black

Summary: A man with the ability to edit memories helps
others mend their lives as he earns a second chance for
his own life. Genre: Magical Realism

ISBN 978-1-7355969-2-1 Paperback

ISBN 978-1-7355969-3-8 E-Book

For Kenny

Chapter One

David

The winter night was clear, but there was an inky blackness to the air that snuffed out light as soon as it left the car's headlamps. Sharp stars pricked through the veil of the black dome above the earth, but they did nothing to brighten the car's path as the brothers headed home. David and Jamie were exhausted but wired as they started the long drive home from the concert. The tickets were Jamie's eighteenth birthday present from their parents: two tickets to see the Chili Peppers playing a few towns away. A couple of beers at the concert plus the gas the get there was David's gift to Jamie. Three years older, David was in the driver's seat for the 50-mile trip.

"It was awesome to hear all their hits." Jamie smiled as he thought back through the concert. He sat far down in his seat with his knees propped on the dash.

"Yeah, but I was hoping for more of the new Stadium Arcadium album. There are some sick tracks on there," added David as he kept his attention on the road.

"You can't have it both ways, all new stuff, and all the classic stuff too," said Jamie, exhaustion slowing his words.

"Maybe, but wouldn't that be killer?" There was no immediate answer. The conversation began to dwindle as the warmth of the car and the ebbing adrenaline lulled Jamie toward slumber. David smacked himself briskly on both cheeks as the pull of sleep began to steal his focus. The resulting alertness lasted an unfortunately short time.

"C'mon man," he encouraged himself. "It's not that much farther. Just keep your shit together." David rolled down the window hoping the blast of frigid air would refresh him. Jamie moaned a complaint against the cold wind, then hunched his shoulders and turned away but didn't wake up.

"Alright, I got this," David told himself, but a minute later his eyelids couldn't resist the downward slide. "No, I don't got this. Shit!" He shook his head to get try to get his eyes to catch focus. It was too cold to keep the window open for long. Besides the dry wind was burning his already blurring eyes. "Music. Music is the answer," he muttered as he reached for the radio button. "Music is always the answer." The Fray was crooning on about how to save a life when David jerked awake without knowing he'd fallen asleep for a second. "Shit! I'm awake now! Damn!" His heart pounded at the thought of sleeping even for a second behind the wheel. "Okay, concentrate man! Just a few more miles and I can close my aching eyes." But the darkness and the exhaustion from the excitement of singing and dancing in the isles at the concert silently eased away his consciousness.

Then he was flying. Falling in slow motion. The sensation of a dreamlike tumble proceeded stillness and silence before the cold began to creep in. So cold. So black.

"Son! Hey buddy, can you hear me? Don't move. We're gonna get you out. Just be real still. Does anything hurt?"

David struggled to make out mumbled and disjointed sounds. *Are those voices? Am I dreaming? What are they saying?* His mind swirled in confusion. *Is someone talking to me?* He opened his eyes slightly to find red lights throbbing, bathing everything in surreal color and blinding flashes.

"How's your guy?" the Captain asked another EMT over the bedlam of noise. The EMT just gave him a grave look and shook his head slightly.

The Captain leaned close to David and said, "It's okay, son. We're gonna take good care of you. Can you talk?"

"Wha…? What's happening? David slurred, trying hard to open his eyes.

"You've been in a wreck," the Captain answered.

David struggled to understand the confusion around him. He tried to decipher the swirling words, but his head was pounding. He felt like he was tied down when he tried to move. Concentrating hard to assess the condition of his body, it was difficult to separate the sensations of pain from immobility and the shock from having taken such a blow. "A wreck? I was driving…"

"I know. We're going to get you out," repeated the Captain.

David tried to turn and look for Jamie, but a neck brace was being attached.

"Don't try to move your head," cautioned the rescuer. "Can you tell me what hurts?"

"My head. And my legs." David was becoming more cognizant now, "Where's Jamie? Is he okay? Jamie, you okay, man? Jamie!" he called out.

"We're working to get him out too. Just keep your eyes on me and keep talking to me. What's your name?"

"David."

"Okay, David. As soon as we get you untangled from your car, we have an ambulance standing by."

"An ambulance?!"

"Yes, you've been in a wreck," the Captain repeated calmly.

"A wreck? Where's Jamie?" Panic was beginning to replace befuddlement in David's voice.

"We're working to free him too. I'm going to cover you with a blanket while we cut the car open. It will be loud, but don't worry. I'm right here with you."

The cacophony of shouts, sirens, radios, and equipment ate the desperate calls to his brother out of the air. David couldn't tell whether Jamie had replied or not. He couldn't even be sure Jamie had heard his calls. *Hopefully, Jamie can ride in the ambulance with me. Worse case, I'll see him at the hospital. God, Mom and Dad are going to be pissed!*

Chapter Two

Rommey

Rommey Clipper surveyed the customers of the coffee shop while he marinated in the heavenly scent of fresh brew on the dreary Monday morning. Vacant faces were jonesing for caffeine and maybe some carbs to launch them into their week with purchased vigor.

Geez, we're pathetic. All of us queuing up for sustenance like it was a soup line. Reaching the head of the line to place his order, Rommey recognized Leslie who was packing grounds into the espresso machine. She looked right past him when she turned to pour another customer's order. Of course, Leslie didn't remember him. They never did.

With coffee and paper finally in hand, Rommey squeezed out of the place past the other bleary-eyed patrons dutifully waiting in line for the day's pre-requisites as he exited with his prize. The somber day felt less so after the first sip of the elixir of life. Walking the few blocks to his office seemed infinitely more manageable once the caffeine began to course through his bloodstream, exciting his brain's receptors. Maybe he could face the pile of manuscripts waiting for him, after all.

"Hey Reddy, you ready to take on the day?" he asked the orange tabby who had waited outside the coffee shop and was now tagging along at his side." I bet you can't wait to get started on your morning nap."

Shortly, they arrived at the main door of his forlorn office building. It had been beautiful in its day, and still could be if someone took care of it. The two-story building of red brick was topped with a decorative cornice as was the style in the late 1800s. Rommey leaned back as he pulled open the heavy wood and glass door to admit Reddy, then himself. A directory just inside the door listed several small businesses:

- Alvin Weinstein, Esquire #101. Alvin was a young patent attorney. Rommey had seen him often enough to know his name. What he had never seen were clients entering or leaving his office.
- Giametti Solutions #102. It seemed likely that Mr. Giametti was a mob middle manager from the looks of his visitors.
- The Subtle Sleuth, Private Investigations # 201. Considering the age of the building, Rommey half expected to see a dame with a fox stole over her shoulder slinking out of the P. I.'s door followed by Sam Spade in an overcoat and fedora.
- Lavomer L. Lacer, Editor #202. The building super still hadn't changed the name on Rommey's office listing.

A slightly musty odor common to old buildings enveloped the lobby. The scent of old carpet, dry wood, and ancient varnish from a time when someone cared about the woodwork, mixed to form this space's unique and familiar odor.

Reddy bounded up the steps ahead of Rommey. Climbing the steps, Rommey reached his office door. The gold lettering on the glass read simply:

ROMMEY CLIPPER
EDITOR

This office had been used by editors as long as the building had been standing, from what he was been told. The last editor was Lavomer L. Lacer, as the glass in the door said before Rommey had it re-lettered with his name. Inside, a sagging sofa woefully greeted visitors in the waiting area. He had given up trying to decide if the original color was black or brown. On sunny days, when the large windows lent the room an almost cheery look, the sofa appeared to be dark brown. But on drizzly days like today, he decided, not for the first time, that the sofa was faded black. In the low light, there was nothing to mask the drear of the old space.

Rommey set his newspaper and coffee on the corner of his enormous, ornate desk. It was definitely the nicest piece of furniture in the office. His predecessor and maybe those before him had left the desk in place when they moved out. The desk likely wasn't left out of kindness or generosity, but because it was too big to move. However, the previous occupants hadn't left much else furniture-wise. Some would say the place had a dreary, worn out look, especially on such a drab day. Rommey, however, found it comforting – like an old pair of jeans.

Settling into his worn but comfortable leather chair, he pulled toward him a stack of manuscripts waiting to be edited while he wondered what real work the week would bring. Checking his email, he found a request for a sample edit waiting from a potential client. The next email was yet another version of a client's magnum opus, as she obviously considered it. Each time she sent another version she swore, "This is truly *the* final, final revision. Please just dispose of the others."

Gladly. This is, what, the fifth "final" version she's sent? Thankfully he hadn't started editing it, so it didn't matter.

With a tentative knock on the outer door, someone let himself into the reception area and said, "Hello?'

"Com'on in. I'll be right with you," Rommey called out from his inner office as he set the manuscripts to the side.

As Rommey emerged into the reception area, the visitor asked, "Are you Rommey Clipper?"

"That's what it says on the door. Can I help you?"

"This is going to sound weird." The visitor hesitated.

"I've heard a lot of weird things. Try me."

"I have this card with your name on it. Rommey Clipper, Editor. Suite 202. #2 Doover Street, Atlanta, GA 30303. There's no phone number or I would have called."

"I don't have a phone. Hate the interruption. Anyway, you need an editor? Are you a writer?" Rommey casually leaned against the door frame.

"No, that's the weird part. I don't write." He tilted his head as if to bring the confusing situation into better focus.

"Okay…," led Rommey.

"But I keep having these incredibly vivid dreams. About you."

"Me? Well, if you are going to be dreaming about me, I feel like I should at least know your name."

"Oh, I'm sorry. It's Edward. You *are* Rommey Clipper, right?"

"Asked and answered. This is me in all my glory." He spread his arms wide as if for closer inspection.

"Hmm. Here's the thing. You don't look familiar at all, and I had never heard of you until I started seeing your name in my dreams. People in the dreams keep telling me to go see you. I see your name on billboards, and license plates, and on food labels. I dreamed that I ordered 'The Rommey Clipper' at my favorite restaurant." Edward was talking fast in his exasperation.

"I'll admit that's a little odd," Rommey said as he straightened and crossed the reception area toward Edward.

"If that's not enough, I reached into the pocket of my raincoat last week and found your card."

"In your dream?"

"No! Your actual card. This card!" He held it out for Clipper's scrutiny. "So maybe we *have* met, and I just don't remember. Oh, and I thought I had thrown the card away, but there it was again on the hall table, so I stuck it back in my pocket." He fingered the card and read it again as if to make sure he had read it correctly.

"I see," was all Rommey offered. Having heard similar stories many times, he had learned it was best just to let the clients talk their way through their confusion until they resolved that they were in his office of their own volition.

Edward continued with his desperate explanation. "So finally I decided to just come here and see what was up. I don't know. Frankly, I'm not at my best, lately." He pushed his hair off his forehead with his palm and exhaled. "I've got a lot on my mind and things are not going that well." He stopped himself in mid-reflection and dropped his hand back to his side. "But you don't want to hear all of that. Anyway, what kind of office is this?"

"As it says on the door, I'm an editor.

"So, you edit, like, books and things?" Edward asked.

"Yes, like books. And things."

"That must be interesting, getting to read books before they are even published."

"It can be," answered Rommey. "They can be pretty rough when I get them. People have absolutely no idea what to do, or not do, with a comma these days. But I digress. Tell you what. I have a few minutes to talk. Would you like to sit down?" They crossed the room to the old sofa and took a seat on either side of the orange tabby who was silently watching the exchange.

"Why do I feel like I want to tell you about all of my problems?" Edward asked, half to himself. His face was a portrait of dismay.

"Maybe because I edit those, too."

"Pardon me? You edit problems?" Edward's incredulity was growing.

"The ones involved with memories, yes."

"People have problems from memories?" He angled his body toward Rommey.

"All the time," said Rommey, nodding.

"I don't think I understand." Edward absently reached out to stroke the cat, who luxuriated in the caress.

"Okay. Did anyone ever bully you in school?"

"Sure," answered Edward.

"Made you feel crappy, angry, and scared at the same time. Right?"

"Sure. Just thinking about it makes my stomach kinda hurt, now that you bring it up."

"Exactly. What if you didn't have to remember that?" Asked Rommey.

"I don't know." Edward paused, thinking while he rubbed his palms down his thighs. "I think it taught me to stand up for myself. In fact, I sucker-punched that asshole right in the gut one day at recess when no teachers were looking. He never bothered me again," Edward finished, chuckling at the memory of his triumph.

"What if there were too many bullies, or they were too big, or the teasing went on and on until your self-worth was destroyed for the rest of your life? Might you want to trash those old memories?"

"Yeah, I guess so." The bravado suddenly left Edward's body. "You know, I have a situation like that, well sort of."

"I'm sure you do."

"There was this girl…" began Edward.

"Stop," interrupted Rommey.

Edward's head jerked up at being rudely cut off. Confusion narrowed his eyes.

"You can tell me why it's a problem, but not the details - not yet anyway. Before we go any further, you have to decide."

"Decide what?" asked Edward.

"If you want this memory removed. Edited or clipped, as we call it."

11

"You could do that?"

"Let's assume for a minute that I could. Would you want every memory of this girl wiped clean? Irretrievable?"

"Yes. I mean, I think so...well, maybe," Edward reconsidered his answer.

"When you decide, if you are positive you want the memory gone forever, come back to see me.

"Can I call you with questions?"

"No phone," Rommey reminded him.

"Can I stop by? Or email you?"

Rommey was rising from his chair, encouraging Edward to do the same. "Of course. Until then, think long and hard about the complete removal of this girl from your memory. If you decide to proceed, be advised it is irreversible.

"You can consider your options, but you'll be unable to discuss this opportunity with anyone else. If you try, the thought will immediately evaporate from your mind. But it will return repeatedly until you've made your decision. If you decide to keep your memories of her, you will do so, and every recollection about our encounter will disappear. If you decide to have your memory edited, come back to me. My office hours are eight to five Monday through Thursday, and eight to three on Fridays."

Rommey patted Edward on the shoulder urging the bewildered man slowly toward the door. Rommey heard him mumbling "irreversible" as he trailed away from the office in a daze, as many clients before him had done.

Rommey returned to his desk to dig back into a godawful memoir by a twenty-year-old who hadn't lived long enough to have any insights on life or any original experiences. For some reason, he thought the world needed to hear every morsel of his angst and insights. And incidentally, the writer had no idea what to do with a comma. However, he had paid half the editing fee in advance, so edit the mess, Rommey would. He had rent to pay like everyone else.

Chapter Three

Edward

About a week after Edward found his way to Rommey's office the first time, he returned. The outer door squeaked slightly as it opened. Rommey rose to find Edward standing in the reception area nervously fingering his hat.

"I see you've come back. You've made your decision about the memory, then?" asked Rommey.

"Yes, I have." Nervously darting eyes and restless hands betrayed the apparent confidence in Edward's voice. "I mean I think so. How much does this memory editing cost?"

"You mean money?" Asked Rommey.

"Of course that's what I mean. What else would I mean?" Ask Edward. His edginess came across as hostility.

"There is no money required. Consider it a service I provide to my fellow man."

"Well... okay then," Edward said warily.

"Fine then. Come into my office so we can dispense with a bit of business first." Rommey escorted Edward into his private office and seated him across the desk. "There is a sort of contract or disclosure I need for you to sign before we begin."

"Contract? I knew there was going be a hidden charge for this. I knew it! Well, I didn't even bring any money, so you're out of luck, buddy." Edward jumped up to leave before Rommey stopped him.

"Settle down, Edward. Please. Have a seat." Rommey motioned him back into the chair. "It's not like that. There are just some things I need to make sure you understand."

Edward slowly sank back into the chair. "Okay..." Suspicion remained in his voice.

"First take a look at this. If you don't agree to any of these terms, we won't continue. There's no obligation." Rommey handed him an ancient vellum document written in elegant script, which read:

ACKNOWLEDGMENT

I, Edward Widdlefish, (the "Client") being of sound but troubled mind, do willingly and of my own volition request Rommey Clipper ("The Editor") to remove irksome, painful, or other unwanted memories which I will willingly provide. Further, I have had the opportunity to discuss the items below with said Editor and am satisfied that I want to proceed with the editing procedure:

1. *Memories thus removed become the full property of The Editor. No rights reserved.*

2. *This procedure is for subtractions only. There are no additions.*
3. *Under no circumstances may memories be reclaimed by Client, family members, or others at any time.*
4. *All deletions are final.*
5. *In payment for services rendered, Client agrees to pay Editor the sum of one pleasant memory, past or future. Past forfeited memory to be determined solely by Client. Future forfeited memory to be determined by The Editor, his heirs, successors, and/or assigns.*

Note 1: Client will not remember Editor after the procedure.

Note 2: Client may experience mild confusion for a few days after the procedure. This is to be expected and will resolve itself. It will not interfere with Client's ability to complete tasks such as driving. Nor will it interfere with current relationships that are not directly associated with the deletion.

By my signature below, I hereby acknowledge and accept the terms above.

Signed:_____
Date:_____
...because forgiving is difficult but forgetting is impossible.

When Edward had finished reading, Rommey asked, "Do you have any questions? I'll answer anything you like before you sign."

Edward's lips moved as he read the old document a second time which, to Edward's surprise, had his name, first and last, elegantly lettered on it. "So, you can really take out a memory that I don't want anymore?"

"Yes."

"And there is no charge except an old memory?"

"Or a future one. That's correct," assured Rommey.

Edward hesitated, sighed, and finally grabbed the offered quill and signed in a shaky hand. "Are you a therapist or counselor or something?"

As Rommey ushered Edward from the desk to a deeply cushioned chair, he replied, "No, I'm an editor like it says on the door. You tell me about your memory, and I remove it."

Edward scanned Rommey's office looking for reassurance in some object he hadn't spotted yet. "This feels like therapy."

"Quality editing often does." Rommey smiled to himself. He walked behind Edward's chair to check the location of the receiving vessel and to make sure it was open. "I'm confident you are going to get what you are seeking out of our session. Why don't you just tell me about the issue and let's see what we can do." Rommey seated himself across from Edward, leaned forward, and encouraged him to proceed. This was often the hardest part for the client, but once he got them going the memory would roll out on its own. "First, tell me what memory you will forfeit in payment," said Rommey.

"A future one," Edward said without hesitation. "I'm not giving up any of my good memories. If it's a future one, I'll never miss it, right? Do I have to tell you which one? I mean, how can I do that?"

"No, no, we'll take a future memory of our choice. You're sure now?"

"Completely sure," nodded Edward. His growing confidence was evident in his relaxing posture.

Having dispensed with the formalities, Rommey said, "Now what memory is it that you'd like to have deleted?"

Edward fidgeted and wrung his hands as his discomfort rose again, then he began relating his memory. "It's this girl…"

"Of course it is." Rommey chuckled to himself. Painful memories were so often about love.

"I mean, it was a long time ago." A silvery mist of disappointment was just beginning to gather above Edward's head.

"That's okay. Go on," Rommey encouraged. He almost had him now. A couple more sentences and the rest would pour out like water from a tipping cup.

"She came to my high school when we were sophomores. I know it seems stupid to be talking about it now. I'm a grown man!"

"This is obviously important to you or you wouldn't be here." Rommey consoled him.

"Right." Edward paused to think, then said, "I never got to date her because another guy got her attention first and they dated right through school, eventually getting married. I mean I guess I'm happy for them, but I can't stop comparing every woman I meet to her. No other woman has ever measured up. Yeah, I realize that I've turned her into some kind of perfect creature that she probably never was, but I can't get past it. I'm still alone with no hope of that changing as long as I can remember her."

"I understand. Tell me about her."

18

Edward broke out of his remembrance to question Rommey again. "How does this work, anyway?"

Rommey sighed and tried to get Edward back on track before the moment was lost. "Let me worry about the mechanics of it. You won't feel a thing, or no more than you let yourself feel, anyway."

"I'm not sure I like the sound of that." Edward gripped the arms of the chair, ready to rise and bolt.

"Look, you can feel the emotion of the memory, but there is no pain from me. Okay? We can't stop now. You've agreed to the terms and you've started telling me your memory. You really must keep going."

"And if I don't?"

"You won't like it," Rommey replied calmly hoping his demeanor was contagious.

"Why is that?" Edward raised his voice as the edge of panic began to creep in.

Rommey sighed. "So many questions for this stage of things, Ed. You should have asked all your questions before we started." Rommey then refocused to answer Edward's question. "You won't like it because if we don't get the whole memory, it can leave a leak."

"A leak? What does that mean?" Edward tilted his head to the side and furrowed his brow, growing more anxious.

"Let's say you could lose a lot of memories you didn't intend to. Or everything."

"Everything?!" Edward nearly shrieked.

"Yes, everything."

"What happens then?" His eyes were wide with mounting hysteria.

Rommey was reluctant to say it, but full disclosure was part of the deal. If people asked, he was required to answer truthfully. "They call it amnesia when it is a big leak and a client loses everything quickly. A smaller leak is basically dementia."

"You mean like Alzheimer's?"

"That's what I'm saying," Rommey replied flatly. "Now can we con-"

"But…I didn't understand…" Edward was fully panicking now.

"Look, take a deep breath, Edward. You're fine," Rommey nearly purred. "I'm very careful. As long as you give me the whole memory, we can make very tidy work of this. I don't mess up. I've never left a leak, but you have to do your part."

"I don't guess I have any choice at this point, do I?" Rommey could see a vein throbbing on the side of Edward's throat. His breath was coming in pants.

"No, you really don't. Just relax and continue," said Rommey calmly. "It will be fine. Now tell me about this girl. What was her name?"

During a troubled pause, several emotions passed across Edwards's face. Finally, he resigned himself to the task, tightly closing his eyes and continued. "Her name was Emma," he said unsteadily. "That's what most of us called her anyway. Her real name was Emmalee, Emmalee Hudgens. She was beautiful." His voice calmed at the mention of her name.

"Of course she was. Tell me more about her."

"She was from a small town in South Georgia. Some people made fun of her accent I but thought it was cute. So sweet." Edward's voice was becoming drowsy, almost trance-like as his memory took him back through the years. His breathing slowed. "She was perfect. Kind. Sort of quiet. And beautiful. Did I tell you she was beautiful?"

"Yes, you did," Rommey replied stifling a yawn. While Edward detailed his every memory of Emma through three years of high school, Rommey checked

20

around the side of the chair to make sure the memory was exiting Edward properly. The silvery vapor flowed smoothly from Edward's scalp down to the receiving vessel sitting behind the chair. Everything was proceeding perfectly. All Rommey had to do now was listen and make sure little Eddie stayed on track. Rommey didn't want him clipping corners of other memories that needed to stay in place, or heaven forbid pulling out whole chunks of one. That was so tedious to repair.

Edward prattled on, "I thought graduation would be my last chance to tell her how I truly felt, but she was busy with her family, and her boyfriend, and then his family...I finally gave up. After that summer, I went off to college and was busy with the typical stuff.

"When I saw Emma's wedding announcement in the paper a couple of years later, I thought I could finally move on. Any chance with her was completely over at that point, you know? However, here I am, still thinking 'what if'. She was so beautiful. Did I tell you she was beautiful?"

"Yes, you did," Rommey replied. Sensing that the memories had all been forfeited, he quietly rose from his chair and said, "Okay, Edward. You just stay put a moment and I'll be right back with a cup of tea for you. You just close your eyes and rest a bit."

Edward mumbled his assent and slumped lower in the soft chair.

Rommey scooped up the vessel from the floor, sliding the cap into place with one smooth movement. A few minutes later, he returned with a cup of tea.

"Here you are, Edward. Some nice hot tea."

"But I don't like tea." Edward pouted like a child before opening his eyes.

"You'll like this, I promise. Now drink up." Rommey encouraged.

Edward looked unconvinced but timidly tried a sip. "Oh, it's yummy!" his eyes opened and lit up.

They are kind of cute during this part. I don't know what it is about a memory dump that turns them into children for a few minutes. Dendrites rewiring, I guess. "I'm glad you like it. I hope you enjoyed your trip to the park today. Napping in the shade all afternoon must have been very restful," Rommey suggested.

"Yes, it was beautiful," Edward replied drowsily.

Almost done here. And one edit closer for me, thought Rommey.

~~~~~~

Edward found himself turning into the parking spot in front of his apartment wondering why he didn't quite remember the drive home from work. *Oh, that's right, I took a vacation day.* He had a vague notion of napping in the park. *I feel so rested.* Then a strange thought overtook him. *I would love a cup of tea.*

Chapter Four

Jenny

Rommey was busy at his computer, editing a compelling short story about finding love in the time of the Syrian refugee crisis when he heard a rustling in the reception area. "Be with you in a second," he called out before finishing the rest of the paragraph. Rising, he walked to the doorway and stuck his head around the doorframe. "Can I help you?"

"Are you Mr. Clipper?" a slight woman asked quietly.

"I am," answered Rommey.

"I heard you might be able to help me."

"Possibly. How did you hear about me?"

"Mia? She's my healer – my counselor, you might say," answered the woman.

"Oh? I don't get many referrals." *Not the human kind, anyway.* Rommey entered the room. "Maybe we can talk for a moment. Would you like to sit down? I didn't get your name."

"Oh, sorry, it's Jenny." They shook hands and took their seats.

"You said your counselor referred you?"

"Well, Mia didn't actually refer me, but she has been helping me work my way through… well, through some old scars. But recently, I've gotten stuck, you might say, in my progress with therapy. When that happened, I started hearing your name. Sometimes on the radio, but not like a regular ad. The announcer literally said my name. 'Jenny. See Rommey Clipper. He can help you.'" She said in an affected voice. "It was so weird. Then I dreamed the same thing. When I saw the billboard with your address, I took it as a sign. Especially when I saw the line that said, 'This means you, Jenny!' It was literally and figuratively a sign!" She laughed despite her distress.

He chuckled. "Things can get a little heavy-handed at times."

"Am I going crazy or can you help me with my memories like I keep hearing and seeing? This must sound crazy." She was growing flustered. "Is there honestly something you can do for people with bad memories? I mean, your door says 'Editor', not 'Psychic' or whatever."

"Yes, I do help people with their memories. Tell me a little about your situation." Rommey encouraged.

"It's embarrassing, frankly. I have memories that are ruining my life." She paused and pressed her lips together before deciding to continue. "My ex thought it was entertaining to beat the shit out of me regularly." She grimaced, maybe at the admission or maybe at the memory of being hit. Rommey wasn't sure which.

He reflexively closed his eyes for a second imagining the assault. "I'm so sorry."

"So am I. Sorry I didn't get out sooner. Sorry I was stupid enough to think I could fix him or be good enough that he wouldn't want to hit me again. Sorry I ever met him." Jenny sighed.

"You don't seem stupid to me."

"Thanks. I just don't know anymore. He told me how stupid, careless, and inconsiderate I was so often, I started to think he must be right. When you live with someone like that long enough, you start to believe all the trash they throw at you."

"So, you want me to remove those memories?" Rommey asked.

"Do you think it will help me? I don't even trust myself anymore," she squirmed. "I'm too scared to try to look for a job. Who would hire me? And if I found a job, what if I couldn't do it? I'm just…"

Rommey broke in as she was starting to dissolve into a puddle of self-doubt. "I said, do you want me to remove those memories? They sound pretty toxic."

"Could you?" she sat a bit straighter and turned toward him.

"Yes, I can. You won't remember him at all."

"That would be incredible," she exhaled her relief.

"However, you need to consider what that means. For example, what if he sees you and tries to get you back? You won't remember what evil he holds."

"I've had a lot of therapy. I know what red flags to look for." She stopped, and her eye widened. "This won't remove what I've learned in therapy will it?"

"No, no. Only the memories you don't want will be subtracted."

"Whew, that's a relief. It has taken a lot of work to get where I am. Back to your question about my ex trying to get back with me, I have different friends now. They'd never let someone isolate me like he did," Jenny answered.

"Will your friends bring him up in conversation?" Rommey asked.

"Mia suggested I tell them never to mention him to me again. It's part of my healing process."

"I see. You're sure, then? Absolutely no memory of him will remain and it can't be restored."

"Absolutely," she said.

Rommey saw confidence in her eyes for the first time, or maybe it was hope. "I have time now if you'd like to go ahead. If you are unsure at all, you can go think about it and come back later."

"There's nothing to think about. I need this evil pox out of my soul." Jenny replied with conviction.

"I don't do souls. Just memories," Rommey smiled kindly, "but I hear what you're saying. If you'll join me in my office, we can get started.". Without hesitation, she signed the yellowed vellum with her full name engraved on it. He seated Jenny in the editing chair where she settled in comfortably. He then quietly slid the uncapped vessel into place. Relaxation changed her whole demeanor. She was almost unrecognizable when the tension left her face. Rommey glimpsed a bit of the unfettered young woman she could be.

Jenny leaned her head back with her eyes closed. "So, what do we do? Is it happening yet?"

"First, per the agreement, you have to decide whether to give me a past or future happy memory. What do you think?"

"Other than the bad years of being with my ex, I've had a good life, so I can think of one to give up." She twisted her mouth while she thought for a moment. "I've got it. I used to love to fish with my grandpa. We went lots of times, so I can spare one of those memories. It was pretty much always the same thing. It wasn't really about catching fish, although we did pull in a good number of bream over the years. The time we shared was always special – just the two of us. We talked about little things…or didn't talk at all. It was just good to be together. I think forgetting just one of those days would be okay. Grandpa would understand. He would want me to be free from that monster."

Rommey smiled to himself at the idea of the little girl and her grandad hanging out together. The pang in his belly reminded him how much he missed his family. He pushed the thought away and took a deep breath. "Now, you just tell me about the things you want to forget. It's the last time you'll ever have to think about them."

"I'm more than ready," Jenny said with conviction. "Here goes. We met at the nursery where he stocked shelves, unloaded trucks, and helped customers. You know, the normal kinda things. I was looking for fertilizer for the pots of flowers at my apartment. I like having beautiful things around me so I'm always planting something. So, um... Dwayne...uh, I hate even saying his name. Anyway, Dwayne was cute and sweet and said all the right things. Except I can't think of him as handsome anymore. Have you ever noticed how someone cute looks even more frightening when they turn mean? You just don't expect it, I guess. Their attractiveness is perverted."

"Yes, I've noticed that," he replied quietly trying not to break her flow of memories. "You're doing fine. Keep going." The brown mist of regret was just starting to collect above her head, gathering itself to flow toward the vessel.

Jenny continued, "We dated about a minute before we thought it would be a great idea to move in together. At first, he was so sweet and attentive. He would check on me and ask when I would be home from work. I thought it was a sign of caring, of love even. Then the questions became about who I was with and why and how long I'd be there and what we were doing and talking about. Over time, too much time," she frowned at the remembrance, "I began to figure out it was all about control.

"Then he proceeded to get my lease changed into his name so I wouldn't have to *worry* about remembering to pay it. It wasn't like I had ever been late paying my rent.

27

Then he made me hand over my paycheck so he could make sure my part of the rent was paid. He said he knew better how to manage *our* money. So, at that point, he had control of my home and my money. That's when he had me pull away from my friends. He said he didn't think they were a good influence on me. How incredibly condescending! But I did what he said just to keep the peace with him. Once I was isolated, the real mental degradation began. It started with second-guessing everything I did. Why did I buy 95% lean ground beef instead of 85%? I was accused of squandering money. If I had bought the 85%, he would accuse me of trying to kill him with the extra fat."

The gray mist of humiliation was flowing now, edging out the brown vapor.

"When I forgot to buy his beer once, he was so enraged that he grabbed me by both arms and shook me so hard I chipped my front tooth. I had to save up money in secret for over a year to have it repaired. Sneaking the money was stupid since he noticed right away when the tooth was fixed. That time he punched me in the jaw. He said it was to break enough teeth that I could never afford to have them all fixed. Then he kept telling me how ugly I was with a giant bruise on my face."

The mist leaving her head was a vile greenish-gray like infection tinged with the black of terror. There was even a slightly foul odor to it, or maybe that was Rommey's imagination. Real or imagined, it turned his stomach.

"That kind of thing went on and on. He drank constantly, then complained about how much I spent on groceries. I started to believe I *was* stupid. I mean I must be to have stayed with him, right?"

Rommey shifted uncomfortably in his seat as his heart pounded in this throat. Fury at this asshole welled up within him, but he had to remain calm and quiet so as not to break the flow. He answered as calmly as he could, "No, you are not stupid. You somehow managed to save yourself."

"Well, I started to believe he was right: that I always made the wrong decisions, that I couldn't be trusted with money and all the rest. He told me that all the time. Sometimes in quiet, snide little remarks, and sometimes so loud and long that the neighbors complained.

"I lost my will – my will to fight back, my will to escape, even my will to eat. He loved the taunt "Skinny Jenny", she huffed with derision. "Eventually, I lost my will to live, so I took a handful of sleeping pills. I wasn't really trying to kill myself. I just wanted all the hate and name-calling and disappointing him to stop for a while. I just wanted to sleep in silence and feel nothing – no fear, no regret, no hopelessness. Dwayne found me passed out and, surprisingly, he called an ambulance."

Though Rommey knew there were other horrors, likely more than could be recounted or even remembered, Jenny didn't need to detail them all. The recollections would cling together and be pulled out like a spider's web, removing the whole cancerous mass. She had told him enough.

"Once my stomach was pumped and I was conscious again, a counselor was there to talk about the unusual number of bruises they found on me. There were new ones and old ones and evidence of other old injuries as well. Thankfully, before I left the hospital, arrangements were made for a spot for me at a women's shelter and I had an appointment with Mia."

Rommey scribbled down the comment about Mia so he could untangle Jenny's relationship with her from the memories she wanted to omit. He was glad to see there was no red mist of anger exiting her. She needed to hold on to that for self-protection. The mist was decreasing now as the last wisps of foul memories left her. "That's very good, Jenny. I think we're finished here."

"Okay," Jenny mumbled dreamily as she drifted off. Her work was done. Her body and mind were rid of the life-sucking memories. Rommey could see the healing beginning by the relaxation in her body. Rising to cap the bottle before any of the evil could find its way out, he proceeded to the tiny kitchen to make tea.

Some of these stories were so hard to hear. It was impossible not to be sickened and infuriated by someone who preyed on another, especially in the guise of love. This clown, Dwayne, could have had a beautiful relationship with Jenny, but he turned it into a scar that had to be excised to heal properly. Thoughts of a relationship he'd like to have once his Editor commitment was completed started to creep in around the edges of his conscious, but he tucked them away for later consideration. Right now, he needed to finish up with Jenny.

She napped comfortably in the chair until Rommey touched her lightly on the shoulder. "Jenny? Hello," he called softly. "I have some tea for you."

"Tea? Oh boy, what kind?" she roused and asked hopefully like a small, drowsy child.

"Chamomile for you," he answered, then added quietly, "and peppermint to ease my sickened stomach."

"Is there honey? Mommy always makes tea with honey," she asked, more awake now, pushing herself up to sit straighter.

"Why, yes, there is." Honey with its drawing properties would remove any broken tendrils of memories too small to have moved out of her body with the mist. "Take your time. You have your whole life ahead of you," he added soothingly.

Chapter Five

Lavomer

Rommey enjoyed the rare experience of sitting with a friend over coffee. Not a friend from his former life, but the one person in his current life who always remembered him. They were alone on the coffee shop patio in the middle of the afternoon, so they could speak comfortably.

"So Lavomer. When are you going to explain everything about how The Editor works?" asked Rommey.

"Obviously, you know how it works. You've been editing for a while now," answered Lavomer, somewhat disinterested. "Have you seen what men are wearing to work these days? Golf shirts. Not suits like a respectable human, but golf shirts! Are they golfing in the office? I think not. It's sad how things continue to degenerate. Honestly, I…"

Rommey interrupted, "I know how it works when *I* edit, but how does it work for me?"

"Oh, I suppose it *is* time I explain a bit more," Lavomer answered wearily, turning his attention to Rommey. He breathed deeply and began, "As you know, when you committed suicide…"

"Because you didn't get to me soon enough."

"Yes, yes. I've apologized for that," retorted Lavomer.

"And I've accepted your apology," answered Rommey.

"Then why do you keep bringing it up?" He paused and sighed. "Anyway, because of our, um, miscalculation, you have been given the opportunity to earn back a life."

"By editing. Right. I'm up to sixteen. Only fourteen more to go. Then I'll have my 30 years back," said Rommey.

"Good, right. Now, where were we? Oh yes, you and your situation. As you may or may not recall—no pun intended—upon your, um, demise," Lavomer tilted his head slightly to emphasize his less objectionable word choice, "you went to the pool of potential future editors."

"That part is pretty fuzzy. I don't remember much about it," said Rommey.

"You were placed there while you healed to the point that you could decide whether to return as an Editor or to proceed on. When *I* earned my life back, you were in a position to take my place. Right place, right time, and all like that," Lavomer added with a dismissive wave of the hand.

"Forgive me for not asking before. Are you enjoying your new life?"

"Quite."

"Did you decide to keep your old memories or use material from some of the ones you collected?" asked Rommey.

"That's none of your business," said Lavomer stiffly.

"Oh sorry," Rommey sipped his coffee to hide his embarrassment over prying.

"Have you thought about what you'll do about your memories—stay with the old ones or spin the wheel, as it were, and take new ones?" asked Lavomer.

"Yeah, I've thought about it a lot. I haven't decided, but I have a while yet."

"So, when you get to that point, you'll make your decision: either your memory will be left as is or it will be replaced by bits of others stitched together by the Editorial Council. Then you'll take on a new life and whatever name you want...except your old one, of course," added Lavomer.

"I can't go back to my old name?"

"Of course not. After all, you *died*," he emphasized. "And you can't go back to your hometown looking like you, either! We don't change appearances. You will need a new name and a new home for obvious reasons."

"Wait, so your name isn't Lavomer anymore?"

"Of course not. That was never my real name. It was my Editor name."

"I've gotten used to Rommey Clipper. Can I keep it if I want?"

"Yes, of course. You made it up. It's yours," answered Lavomer.

"It's pretty clever, you have to admit."

"Yes, well...," growing impatient, "you can do as you like about the name issue."

"Wait, I have another question," said Rommey. "Once I finish my edits, I'll be free to live however I want?"

"Well, you have a responsibility of occasional welfare checks on the new Editor, like I'm doing now, but yes, you can do whatever you want with your second chance."

"A second chance," said Rommey as he stared wistfully into his coffee. "I'll try not to screw it up next time."

"Yes. Please." Lavomer replied.

Chapter Six

Gustov

A bear of a man who filled the doorway let himself into Rommey's office. Finding no one in the reception area he turned back and knocked twice on the wooden door. The knock from the ham sized fist resounded through the office startling Rommey from the draft he was trying to edit into something comprehensible. Instilling any kind of grace or cleverness to this work would have to come several edits down the line, if ever, but that would have to wait, for now.

Rommey entered the outer office to find a ruddy-skinned giant of a man with fading red hair standing where a receptionist's desk should be been.

"Hello, may I help you?" Rommey asked.

"I'm sorry to disturb you," he said with a faint German accent. "I'm looking for Rommey Clipper."

"I'm Rommey. And you are?"

"Gus. Well, Gustov, actually. Gustov Heinrich."

Rommey extended his hand. "What can I do for you, Gus?"

"I have this card. It is yours, yes?" Gus held it out for Rommey inspection.

"Yes, that's my card."

"I keep finding it in my pockets, on my counter, on my desk. It says, 'Forgetting is impossible'. Do you think that's true?"

"It is for most people. And unfortunately, the worse the memory is, the less likely it can be forgotten," replied Rommey.

"That is true, I think." Gus paused, slipping his hands into his pockets, gathering his thoughts. "I don't know how to ask you this."

"Just say it. I bet it won't surprise me," encouraged Rommey.

"Do you make bad memories disappear?"

"I can, yes. It depends on the circumstance."

"But how?" asked Gus. His search for understanding of how such a thing could be true contorted his face.

"It's not possible to explain. But when people are so haunted by certain memories that it degrades their life, I can help them forget those memories."

Gus' mouth twisted as he considered this info. "And this is no joke? No trick?"

"No joke. No trick," answered Rommey.

Gus continued his questions. "I understand that if something bad was done to you, you are entitled to forget that."

"Agreed," said Rommey, shifting his weight and thinking he really must get some chairs for the reception area.

"But what about the person who was the bad guy, the guy who did the bad thing? Can *he* be allowed to forget?" asked Gus as he fingered the card he had returned to his pocket.

"He can." Rommey answered slowly wondering just want kind of guy he was dealing with. "Why don't you tell me about it. Not the details, but the basics."

Gus' struggle with the idea played in his eyes. "Might we sit while I tell you my story?" asked Gus.

"Of course. I'm sorry for my poor hospitality. Please…" He motioned Gus to the shabby sofa. Rommey slid Reddy toward the middle so they could sit on either end. Reddy simply purred, raised his chin for a momentary scratch, and settled his head back on his paws to continue his nap.

"When I was *kleiner junge*, a little boy, as I would later learn to translate, my father worked for an international company that moved us to the U.S. We were very excited of course, but it was quite an adjustment. I had some exposure to English in Germany, but here, of course, English is full time. There was no one to help me translate if I got stuck or didn't understand the teacher's instructions. In my new school, I was scared and lonely, plus I felt stupid because English is very difficult. It was exhausting to struggle to speak and understand English all the time. Plus the games, and the jokes, well, everything was different than what I was used to. These things are no excuse, mind you, but that was the origin of my… how do you say, predatory behavior."

"Predatory?" asked Rommey.

"I was a bully. A very large bully," confided Gus with shame. "I was only acting out of fear, trying to throw the first punch, as you say. Is that right?"

"Yes, that's the phrase."

"That doesn't make it right, of course. Memories of my actions then are still painful to me. I have tried to find the children who suffered at my hand, but despite years of trying, I haven't found them all. I think I have done what I could to make amends. Do you think I am justified in letting go now?" asked Gus.

"Do you think you would bully people again? Take advantage of weaker people?" It was not Rommey's job to be judge and juror, but he was curious.

"Ach, no, I am a changed man. I have a degree in social work and have spent the last twenty-five years helping people in need. My agency helps disabled people find resources and we help people to get into drug treatment programs. We help abused women find safe shelter and daycare, so they have a chance to put their lives back together. I often see people on the worst day of their lives, and we help them through it. It is such fulfilling work. I am blessed to have the opportunity to help others."

"Sounds to me like you are entitled to let go of those old memories," said Rommey.

"You think so?

"I do."

Gus let out a long sigh. "That is such a relief to me. I would like to be free of this old shame." Relief relaxed his face, then his brows drew together again. "How does it work? Is there medicine? Or hypnosis?"

"No, it is even easier than that," replied Rommey. "All you have to do is tell me the memories, and I will dispose of them."

"It is that easy?

"Yep."

With that assurance, Gus was eager to proceed. Rommey invited Gus into his inner office to address the pre-printed Acknowledgment, including "Gustov Heinrich" in flowing script.

"You can ask me anything before we start. I'll give you a minute to go over the information," Rommey said as he stood near Gus' chair.

Gus concentrated on the elaborately lettered parchment and read carefully. It has my name on it even though I just arrived?"

"Yes." Rommey answered simply.

Gus raised his brows in question, but receiving no further explanation, he continued, stopping midway. Turning the vellum toward Rommey, he pointed to the middle of the page. "I find this one troubling."

"Can you translate it for me? I can't read German," said Rommey.

"But you happen to have a form in German?"

"The form is available in every language. It is imperative that each person understand exactly what he or she is agreeing to."

Gus shook his head in wonder. "It says I won't remember you." His expression was troubled.

"That's right."

"Why not?"

"Think about it. If you remember me, you'll wonder from where? If you figure that out, you might remember what we did here. If you do that, it would be very confusing for you since you won't remember the memories we clipped. You might come back repeatedly to ask a lot of questions with unsatisfactory answers. It's better this way, believe me," explained Rommey.

"I see." Gus thought for a moment. "But I won't even be able to say, 'thank you'?"

"Nope. No one does."

"That's too bad. Then I shall say 'thank you' in advance. You are doing me a great service," Gus rose and grabbed Rommey into a giant's hug.

"No problem," Rommey whispered as he tried to breathe in the bear's embrace. When he was released to recover his breath, he said, "Ready?"

"Absolutely."

When Gus had moved to the editing chair, the yellow mist of cowardice mingled with wisps of brown regret started to gather around his scalp even before he began his story. The memories seemed anxious to leave. Rommey prepared the vessel and took his seat to hear Gus' memories – a good one along with the troubling ones.

Chapter Seven

Jake

Rommey sat down in front of his computer to dig into a new editing project. Dolores Finkleburn, pen name Sweetie Amore, author of *A Billionaire for Christmas* and *The Baron's Birthday Gift,* had submitted another of her "clean, sweet, romances" for him to proofread. Thankfully, he was only looking for typos and grammatical errors since reading her story for content with its saccharine and predictable plot was a task he did not relish.

"Wanna make a bet before I open it, Reddy?" The cat stared at Rommey with apparent interest. "I'm betting small-town girl runs into an old high school acquaintance, no wait, an old flame, who's back from the big city to take care of his mom, his grandma, his old dog, or his inherited property. They spark, but they hate each other. Then they are forced to work together on some town project and fall into everlasting love." Reddy did not seem eager to take the bet, so Rommey turned back to his screen. "Let's see how close I am."

Sarah Jane was about to finish her day at the hardware store she inherited from her dad when the bell on the front door jingled. "Be right with you!" she called from the storeroom.

"Sure, no rush," the tall, dark-haired customer answered. While he waited, he perused the bulletin board advertising local fresh eggs, a lost chocolate lab, and rabbit kittens for sale. Most of the notice board was covered by a poster for the upcoming fair to raise money for a new playground.

"That's where they'll be forced to work together. Check! Told ya!" gloated Rommey. Reddy appeared unimpressed.

Sarah Jane appeared out of the back, wiping her hands on her clerk's apron. Her crystal blue eyes looked up into the customer's dazzling green ones. "Bruce!" she exclaimed when she immediately recognized the customer. His face was more mature now, more chiseled, but there was no mistaking the man, or the bit of rage that flared back to life in her chest.

"Bingo! Am I good at this or what, Reddy?" Reddy slowly blinked his reply.

Hatred immediately clouded her pretty face.

41

"Sarah Jane!" an arrogant smirk formed his full lips into a mocking sneer.

"So here we go. Only 250 pages, a misunderstanding, and a giant fight until true love sweeps them both away into everlasting bliss, Reddy! Aren't you excited?" Reddy turned away and padded off to find a quieter place for a nap. "Sheesh, I'm spending way too much time alone," mumbled Rommey.

A message pinged as it arrived in Rommey's email box just as he was settling in to Sarah Jane's tempest:

> Dear Mr. Clipper,
>
> I am seeking an editor for a book about my military experiences as a sergeant in the U.S. Army. This is my first book and I understand that a developmental edit would be useful. Please let me know if you do that kind of editing and if you would be interested in working with me.
>
> Thank you, Jake Gipson

At least this person has had some life experience and probably has a story to tell. It will certainly be better than the, "Memoir of a Very Average Life All the Way to Age Twenty" *that I've been working on or Dolores Finkleburn's romance novel.* Rommey responded:

> Dear Mr. Gipson,

If you are going to be in the Atlanta area, I would welcome the opportunity to meet with you.

R. Clipper, Editor

Soon, Rommey received a response:

I have completed my enlistment and now lived in Marietta. I can come to your office downtown next week if you have time to meet with me. I haven't done this before so I hope you can give me some direction. How does it work? What do I need to bring?

Jake

Rommey replied:

I find the editing process is basically a conversation at this stage. Brings your thoughts and a note pad and we'll talk through your ideas. I look forward to meeting with you.

R. Clipper

Arrangements were made for the meeting at Rommey's office the following week.

"At least I'll have a human to talk to for a while. That will be nice," Rommey mumbled to himself. "Uh, no offense, Reddy-man."

Reddy merely flicked his tail in a mild pique.

~~~~~

That evening Rommey and Reddy walked home the few blocks to his apartment.

"So, Reddy. How was your day?"

"Meow."

"Anything exciting happening under the furniture that I need to know about? Like mice, for example?"

"Meow."

"Well, yeah, I guess you wouldn't know. Mice are not your thing, are they?"

Reddy didn't answer but trotted along like a well-trained dog. Walking up the stairs to the apartment, Rommey unlocked the door. Reddy slipped inside through the first sliver of an opening and headed directly to his bowl.

"Tuna time, is it?"

The responding meow was much more insistent than his earlier casual replies.

"You don't say!" Rommey crossed the small apartment and reached for the refrigerator door. Soon a bit of tuna on a small plate was placed on the floor. "Here ya go, Redactor - or do you prefer Reddy, sir? There was no reply from Reddy except a deep purr as he tucked into the snack. "Don't ruin your dinner!"

Rommey leaned back against the counter and watched in amusement at Reddy devoured his daily spot of fish. He truly was a wonderful companion, but Rommey missed having real friends. Human friends. While he was earning his life back, friends were a difficult complication. He couldn't tell anyone about his past or his family. And a girlfriend was out of the question. But with each memory edit he performed, he was one step closer to being released from his period of service. He truly liked the work of editing—both types. But the isolation was difficult, and he was ready to start building a life again.

"Until then, Reddy, all we have is each other. Enjoy your snack, buddy." Rommey took a beer from the fridge and headed to the sofa to catch up on the day's news.

Chapter Eight

Max

At nearly five in the afternoon, the old door squeaked open. A young man sporting a hoodie, the edges of a tattoo showing just below his cuff, eased into the office. Rommey stuck his head around the door, glasses still down on his nose, and said, "Hi, can I help you?"

"I think so. I mean, I hope so," the young man replied.

Rommey waited for him to continue but the man was occupied in looking around the office at the fixtures, the worn and wavy carpet with a now indiscernible pattern, and the grand window whose top arch matched that of the ceiling.

"Those light fixtures, do you know if they are original to the building?" The man asked.

"I guess so. I mean, I not sure. I haven't given it much thought," answered Rommey.

"These old buildings, the ones from the turn of the century, have so many ornate design elements. Can you imagine designing windows like that now? And stain-grade trim? Wow," the young man continued.

"Are you an architect? Or from the historical society?" Rommey asked.

"No, unfortunately." Sadness replaced his awe while he continued to scan the door frames and hardware.

"Are you writing a book about architecture or something?"

"No. Why would you ask me that?" asked the man.

"Well, you obviously know a lot about buildings, enough to have an appreciation for them on a detailed level, and I'm an editor, so..." he said pointing to the backward letters on the glass door.

"No. Yeah, I've heard you might be able to help me. Well, not 'heard' exactly, more like dreamed, or imagined, or something. I don't know. It's weird," he said, growing flustered.

"How so?" Rommey asked.

"I keep seeing your name. There is a billboard right outside that says, 'Rommey Clipper can help – even you Max.' How weird is that? I thought it was some kind of advertising gimmick."

"Outside my building? Where?"

"I'll show you. It's right outside," answered the man. They walked to the large window and leaned forward, scanning the street below in every direction. There was no billboard below. Not one anywhere to be seen.

"I'll be damned," Max whispered.

"I doubt it," muttered Rommey.

Max didn't hear him, lost in his thoughts as he continued to scan the street. "Anyway, I was down here just walking around looking at old buildings, trying to make myself feel better, clearing my head about things."

"Something bothering you?" asked Rommey.

"Yeah, a lot of things." Max continued to stare out the window. "You might say I've made a lot of mistakes. I wish I could forget them all so I could just go on and not think about what might have been."

"As it happens, I sometimes help people with that kind of problem," offered Rommey.

"Seriously?" Max turned away from the window to face Rommey. His expression was that of a person trying to discern exactly what he was hearing.

"Yep. What I am about to tell you is just between us. If you decline my offer, it is your choice, and you'll have no recollection that it was ever made. You won't even remember that we met, for that matter."

Max took a step back and said, "Okaaay." He was obviously dubious but intrigued.

"I can remove unpleasant, painful, disruptive memories if you like."

Shoving his hands in his pockets for fortitude, Max thought for a moment, then asked, "How does that work? Is this some hinky deal? Some kind of drug thing? 'Cause I'm not into that stuff, brugh."

"No, no, nothing like that. You just tell me the painful memory and I take it away. It will be like it never happened," said Rommey.

"So I just tell you how I squandered my chance at college, my chance to be an architect by not applying myself and partying too much and pissing off my parents until they cut off my tuition, and that regret and remorse will be gone forever?" Max asked.

"Yep. But, wait a second. That's all you did? You are haunted by what might have been?"

"Yeah, I drank too much. I skipped classes and wound up on academic probation not once, but twice. When my grades fell so low, I knew I couldn't recover, I just stopped going. God, my dad was pissed! And my mom. Ugh, she looked so disappointed. That was the worst part, you know? The disappointment." Max lamented.

"Do you still want to be an architect?"

"Yeah, I want to design buildings like this, with warmth and character, instead of those glass and steel monoliths." His eyes glimmered as he turned to gaze back out across the city.

"It doesn't sound to me like you want to forget about that dream."

"No, not the dream," he realized. "Just my stupid ass actions of the past."

"How can you learn from those mistakes, if you can't remember them?" Rommey asked.

Max sighed in resignation. "Yeah, I might just keep making stupid decisions. I've grown up a lot since then, that's for sure, but I not sure I trust myself. If I had a chance to do it all over, I think things would be so different.

"Why can't you?" asked Rommey.

"Why can't I what? Oh, go back to school? How am I supposed to do that?" Max asked with a snort of derision.

"People do it all the time. Start part-time with day or night classes while you work. A class or two a semester at whatever college is convenient. When you get the basic classes out of the way, take out a loan, if you have to, to take the specific classes that are required for your program. There's financial aid for that, too. Dedicated, poor students are eligible for various programs. If you want it bad enough, you'll work out that part.

"You don't need to forget, Max. You need to *remember*. Remember your dreams. Remember that it doesn't take much to derail them. You already know what not to do, so do the opposite. That information is too valuable to forget."

Rommey stood and crossed his arms watching Max staring back at the city through that big beautiful window. He could feel the hope and purpose flicker to life inside Max. He hoped it would grow into a flame of determined commitment. "So, what do you think?"

Max tore his eyes from the city landscape. Rommey could see resolve on Max's face where before there had

49

been defeat.

"I think maybe I'll just hold off on the memory editing thing for now. You've given me a lot to think about. You said if I decide not to do it, I won't remember this conversation."

"That's right."

"Will I forget the idea to try school again?"

"No. That idea was inside you all the time. I just helped you find it. And remember, it's your passion. That won't go away. Besides, if you decide to give it all up and wallow in the bad judgment of your past, your mind will remind you where to find me.

Max twisted his lips in thought, then stuck out his hand to shake Rommey's. "Thank you, Mr. Clipper." He held on to Rommey's hand an extra few seconds before nodding in newfound resolve, then headed out the door.

"See you around, Max…or hopefully not." *Look at me helping someone remember for a change.* Rommey thought. *That's the one clip that got away, and I'm not sorry.*

Chapter Nine

Jake

On the agreed-upon day, Sgt. Jake Gipson arrived at Rommey's office with a pad and pen as advised. Jake was heavily built, still wearing the buzz cut to which he had grown accustomed during his years of service. Though he was wearing jeans and a t-shirt, it wasn't hard to imagine that physique in fatigues, carrying a large firearm.

"Welcome to my office, Sergeant," Rommey said, extending his hand, the man's bearing was all military—rod straight posture and well-muscled readiness. Rommey felt like he should salute.

"Thank you, sir. You can call me Jake. I'm no longer a soldier," Jake offered.

"Ah, well do come in. I'm looking forward to hearing about your work."

As they crossed the office, Jake said, "Calling it a "work" is an overstatement. It's more of an idea at this point."

Rommey smiled and escorted Jake into his office where they sat across the desk from one another. "So, tell me what you have in mind for your book."

"I want to write about a difficult mission that my unit went through in Afghanistan."

Rommey replied, "That certainly sounds like the basis for a compelling book. Can you tell me more about what happened? That is if you feel comfortable sharing the information at this point."

"Sure." Jack cleared his throat and began, "At oh-seven-hundred-hours, my team moved out to take up a position on a hilltop near a village. There was suspicion of HVTs, that's high-value targets, in the area. Our mission was just to watch and catalog vehicles. Simple. No mixing with the locals. No building searches. Just watching. We were all feeling pretty good. On the way to the location, Johnson had burst into his version of *Bohemian Rhapsody* and he had everyone singing along." A lopsided smile crossed Jake's face before it quickly dissolved into a grimace and he stopped talking.

After a moment Rommey said, "Why do you want to write this book?"

Stumped, Jack stammered, "I...I want to get it all down. So the details don't get lost."

"Did the army take a report of facts," ask Rommey.

"Yes, there was a debriefing and an AAR."

"The AAR?" Rommey asked

"Yeh, sorry, the After Accident Report. I prepared it for my C.O. It's all in the copy I brought except for the classified details."

"And did you tell them everything you could remember?"

"Of course. It's my responsibility to provide all the facts," answered Jake, starting to look like a man on a witness stand whose integrity was being questioned.

"But there are more than details you want to preserve." It wasn't a question.

"Yes," Jake's thick shoulders sagged as if the memories weighing on his mind were physically too heavy to bear.

"You need to tell the story your own way? Is that why you want to write the book?" asked Rommey.

"I want to…I need to…," he stopped again struggling to put his thoughts into words. "I need to download this somehow. I hope it will release its hold on me. I have to try something. My shrink suggested that writing about it might help. He didn't say I should publish it, but I figured if I was gonna go to the trouble of writing it all out, I might as well try to do something with it. It's a hell of a story."

"Makes sense," Rommey said. "May I see what you brought with you?" Jake handed him several neatly typed pages with areas blacked out. "I see you have the chronology down. That's an excellent start."

Rommey skimmed the sheet, then said, "I suspect there's a lot more to it than the dry information here."

"Well, sure, but…"

"I also suspect that's the part you want to download," said Rommey.

Jake exhaled sharply and his shoulders slumped. "I can't stop thinking about it. Can't stop going over what happened that day again and again in my mind. I'm obsessed, or maybe haunted is a better word."

"I'm no therapist, but I can help you work through this – the writing part of it, that is. As I said, you have a good start with the chronology. Let's work on fleshing this out a little. Tell me about what life was like there."

Jake's pulled back his large shoulders and visibly relaxed now that things were moving toward a subject without so many difficult emotions.

He and Rommey spent the next two hours talking about the personalities of the guys in his units, their quirks and habits, their inside jokes, as well about the heat, the sand, and ingenious ways to deal with it. By the end of the afternoon, Jake left with an assignment to flesh out the story by first writing about these things.

After he left, Rommey sat in his too-quiet office and watched Reddy chase a fly from window to window. His afternoon with Jake left him with images of camaraderie and making a family out of those around you wherever you are. The absence of his own family still left a painful hollow place in his chest, but he couldn't help but look forward to making a new family of friends once he was free to establish lasting relationships again when his memory editing obligation was complete.

Chapter Ten

Evelyn

At just after eleven in the morning, the soft rustling in the outer office didn't register with Rommey right away. He was concentrating on chapter three of a fantasy tome where magical powers were just beginning to be revealed.

Click, click, click.

He was intrigued as the story unfolded. The writer knew her craft and she even had her grammar in good form.

Click, click.

Though fantasy was not his favorite genre, he was enjoying the world she was crafting in his mind with her descriptions.

Click, click.

Looking up at last, he cocked his head and tried to place the origin of the rhythmic metallic clicking. He rose and peered around the door frame to find a small, older woman knitting away in his sagging sofa with the sun at her back. Reddy was comfortably ensconced on her lap.

"Hello?"

"Hello, dear," she replied, laying her knitting aside. A bright smile lit her soft face and gray eyes behind her reading glasses.

"May I help you?"

"I'm here to have a memory removed," she said matter-of-factly.

"Oh?" Rommey was stunned into a monosyllabic reply by her forthrightness. There was no wondering, no confusion on her part.

"You *are* Rommey Clipper, aren't you?" she continued.

"Yes, ma'am," he continued to be mystified by the woman as he eased his way from his office toward her.

"And you remove memories? Bad ones, I mean?"

"Yes, ma'am," he replied, clasping his hands behind his back as he stopped before her.

She reached down to place her knitting project in her bag. "Well, let's get started. What do we do first?" She tilted her head, brows raised in complete acceptance of this usually foreign idea.

"May I ask you a question?" The whole conversation was backward to the usual approach of Rommey providing the answers, not the questions.

"Certainly, dear."

"Well, two questions actually. First, may I know your name?"

"Oh, yes. How silly of me. I did get ahead of myself, didn't I. I'm just so anxious, you see. My name is Evelyn."

"It's very nice to meet you, Evelyn. My second question is, how did you hear about me?"

"Well, I was thinking about…" she paused a moment to determine how best to explain it. "As I so often do, I was thinking about an *incident*, shall we call it. And I was feeling just awful about it. It plagues me so. If only…" she paused again and released a breath of air, looking wistful. "Anyway, when I put my hand in my apron pocket, I found your card." She read the tag line, '*Forgiving is difficult. Forgetting is impossible.*' Since I've never seen your card before, I knew it was something important. Something

56

special. As I read your card over and over, the thought came to me that must help people forget. That is what I need – to forget. That was yesterday, so today, here I am," she finished brightly.

"I see. Without telling me the details, can you tell me what kind of memory you want to have removed?"

At this, Muriel looked troubled, took a deep unsteady breath, and slowly exhaled. Conjuring the remembrance changed her physical being. Her bright cheerfulness was transformed into pensive sorrow. When she had gathered her thoughts into words, she said, "I saw something terrible," she paused. "A young man took his life and I couldn't stop him. It haunts me. I've tried to tell myself that when a person is determined to do that, you can't save them, but that doesn't do a thing to assuage my guilt and saddness."

Rommey nodded in understanding. "I think I can help you." He eased over to lock the front door and invited her into his office. After the usual explanation of how it worked, she signed the Acknowledgment without hesitation and settled into his comfortable guest chair.

"Have you decided whether to forfeit and old or a future memory?" he asked.

"Oh, there's no question: a future memory. At my age, all my old memories are so precious. Loved ones who are no longer with me, fun times we had, even the difficult time are important for the lessons they taught. I could never part with those. With a future memory, I'll never miss it. Besides, the power- that-be might not get around to harvesting one before I leave this earth!" She smiled with a wink. "One thing is troubling, though. The Acknowledgment said I won't remember you afterward. Normally, I would enjoy feeling grateful for your help, but I do recognize the inherent logical problem in that, so I'll thank you in advance. I wish I had known about that part

57

of it before I came so I could have baked you something special in advance. You will forgive me, I hope."

"Oh yes ma'am. I thank you for your kindness, but it's not necessary."

She looked closely at Rommey for a moment, and said quietly, "Will it hurt? I mean, it's worth it even if it does, but I'd like to be prepared."

"No, ma'am. I've never had anyone act as if it was uncomfortable. Most people become so relaxed that they become quite sleepy by the time we're finished.

"Oh, that sounds very pleasant," she brightened. "Are we ready to begin?"

"Almost." Rommey placed a vessel behind her chair, seated himself across from her. "Okay, here we go. This is the last time you'll ever have to think about this. Can you tell me about what you'd like to forget?"

"Well, it was a lovely spring morning about five years ago. I was driving to my daughter's house to help her out with the new baby. She's just the sweetest thing! She's – "

Rommey broke in, "You mustn't tell me about things you want to remember. Just the bad parts, okay?" He might have to fix that, but it would probably be okay. It was only a small glitch and she was so in love with her grandbaby there were likely millions of thoughts about how much she adored her. She would never miss one. Hopefully, it wouldn't come up again.

"Oh, yes, I definitely don't want to forget her! That's not at all what I'm after." She smiled. "Well, as I passed over the interstate bridge, I saw a man—a boy, truthfully, standing on the outside of the fence. It took me a second to realize what I was seeing. And the traffic was moving so fast. As soon as I got to the other side of the bridge, I looked in my rearview mirror to see if he was, in fact, on the outside of the fence. When I confirmed that he was, I careened off into the grass, threw my car in park, and ran back toward him. There was little room between the lane and wall with the fence on top." She squirmed in her chair as if she wanted to run toward him even now. Her eyes grew wide with terror as she focused on the re-run of events that only she could see.

"It was so frightening with the traffic zooming past. He had climbed over the top of the fence and stood with his back against the fence. He held on by weaving his fingers through the wire behind him. There was virtually nothing for him to stand on. He was just inches from falling onto the traffic below. I called to him over the noise. 'Wait! Please don't hurt yourself. I want to help you.'" She called out now as she replayed the scene. "He just looked at me with cold eyes, so full of pain. 'Too little too late, lady. Mark Fallon is no more!' Then without hesitation, he just let go and fell from his perch into the traffic below. It happened so fast, but oddly, the fall was like slow motion." Goosebumps stood erect on her arms, her face twisting with the pain of the vivid memory, as the white mist of sorrow, and the hot pink puffs of shock mixed with brown wisps of regret poured from her.

"I'm so sorry you had to see all that." Rommey tried to remain calm, but he was truly unsettled by her description of the suicide. His heart pounded in his ears as he experienced not only Evelyn's horror but also the hopelessness and pain of the jumper.

"I'm sure I talked to the police, but I don't remember it. Shock, I guess. I often wonder if I had said something different to the boy or called an expert instead of trying to talk to him myself, maybe it would have turned out differently. I didn't know what I was doing. What if I said the wrong thing, just the thing that made him jump?" She closed her eyes tightly and wept about it for the last time. Deep brown vapor flowed heavily sinking quickly into the jug.

Rommey reached over and held her hand. "There was nothing more you could have done. He was determined, as you said. Shhh." He comforted her. "Let me get you some tea. You rest now." He patted her on the shoulder as he rose.

"Thank you, dear. I think I'll just rest my eyes for a moment," she said as she blotted them with her dainty handkerchief.

Evelyn napped while Rommey tidied up the jug of her memory. He filled the kettle and set it on the burner. *There's so much pain in the world. Why couldn't the jumper have met Evelyn before it was too late to save him? He had no idea how much pain he was causing others with his act.* Rommey felt wearied by the weight of her story. *I'll share some chamomile tea with sweet Evelyn until we both feel better.*

Chapter Eleven

Jacob

The days were lengthening, and the temperatures were rising as spring got its footing and claimed the season. There were no more chill winds and drizzly, gray days of late winter. After work, Rommey put Reddy into his satchel and carried him a few blocks to a park to enjoy the late rays of sunlight. When they arrived, Rommey set him down on the path and Reddy bounded ahead. Just ahead, feeding the birds as usual, sat a man that Rommey had seen there before.

As Reddy approached the man, the pigeons backed off to a safe distance by didn't fly from their known food source. Reddy wound himself around the guy's legs, as Rommey approached.

"I hope he's not bothering you. His name is Reddy."

"He's okay. Pretty cat. I just don't want him to get my birds." He reached down to stroke Reddy's silky, orange fur. "You're not going to bother my birds, are you Buddy?"

"Purrt," Reddy answered.

"He's strictly a tuna man. Now, if a bluefin swims by, we may have to hold him down."

The birdman chuckled and cooed to the milling pigeons. "Yeah, you're a stud, Blake," he complimented the big male bird who dragged his fanned his tail feathers along the concrete and puffed out his iridescent chest.

"Blake?"

"Yeah, That's Blake Shelton. He thinks he's the sexiest man alive," said the bird feeder.

"Funny. Sound like you know them pretty well," said Rommey.

"Yeah, I like to come here where it's quiet. Just the birds and me. They're always happy to see me. No judgment. No bad news, ya know?"

"Yeah. Reddy and I come out here to get some exercise. He's cooped up in my office all day."

"You get to have a cat at work?" the birdman asked.

"I work for myself, so..."

"That must be nice. What kind of work?"

"I'm an editor," answered Rommey. The guys raised his eyebrows in question. "You know, books, articles, things like that?"

"So, you're a brain at English and stuff?"

"I guess, but the grammar is the easy part. You can hire someone, me for example, to correct your errors. The real work of it is the creative part."

"It's amazing how many ways there are to tell the basic stories of humanity," the birdman said.

Rommey eyebrows raised in surprise as he realized he might have found someone who shared his view of literature. "That's right. They say there are, what, six or seven basic stories?"

"Yet the libraries are brimming, and people write new ones all the time," said the bird lover.   Reddy,   having gotten his fill of chin-scratching for the moment, walked over to check the edge of the pond for interesting creatures.

"There is something about humans that drives us to tell our stories, our own way," said Rommey.

"The ones we can bear to tell anyway."

"Oh, I'm Rommey, by the way." He extended his hand.

"Jacob," he said, returning the handshake.

"Everyone plans to write the 'Great American Novel'. Some actually do it," said Rommey. "I help them get to the best version of their work."

They both watched in silence for a few minutes while the birds devoured the rest of the seed Jacob had thrown out.

"Well, I guess that's all for today's show," he said as the birds began to disburse. "I best be on my way, too."

"It was good talking with you. Maybe we'll cross paths again."

"Maybe so. It was nice talking with you, Rommey. See ya," said Jacob.

As Reddy chased imaginary creatures in the grass, Rommey took Jacob's place on the bench and reflected on the kinds of stories people told him. Due to the nature of his work, the stories he heard these days were pretty dire ones. By far, the most prevalent life event that people wanted subtracted were affairs of the heart. Just in the last few weeks, he had clipped three variations on a theme:

There was Heath whose girlfriend had left him. He had been bathing himself in comfort food, the hard country blues-guitar of Stevie Ray Vaughn, and general lethargy for entirely too long. His mournful, pining heart would not let him move on. Starting another relationship was out of the question as long as he could remember the woman who left him. His brain tortured him by replaying scenes of situations he had handled badly. "If only I had done this or said that maybe she would have stayed," Heath had mourned repeatedly. Rommey had mended this particular situation several times now for various people by removing memories of the jilter.

Then there was Courtney. She too was jilted but addressed her pain with reckless sex, excessive drinking, and late-night partying. She was bound and determined to have a great time to compensate for her pain even if it killed her. On the verge of losing her job due to absenteeism and worse, she had come to Rommey to clear out the memories that led to her destructive behavior.

The third love-sick sufferer was Tyler. He had decided it was time to move on from his girlfriend. He had broken it off with her in a respectable way that he felt good about. No fireworks. No drama. No infidelity. However, when he found out that Marissa had moved on and was dating a new guy, Tyler suffered a crushing case of seller's remorse. Few things make something or someone more desirable than the inability to have it or them. Such was the case for Tyler. Even though he admitted that her new guy was a better fit for her, it didn't dampen is remorse and jealousy. In Tyler's case, he didn't want to forget the girl, only the knowledge of her new boyfriend. Rommey tried to reason with Tyler about the deficit of logic in this approach, saying, "next time you call her and her new boyfriend answers, you'll be right where you are now." In the end, Rommey had convinced him to go home and think about whether he wanted to forget the girl or just the new guy and the pain of knowing about him. He invited Tyler to return when he had come up with a more workable plan.

*There's so much pain in the world. My own included. At least I can take some of it away for other*s. He was still unsure whether he would keep his old memories when he had a chance to make that decision. *Maybe it's a case of 'the devil you know is better than the devil you don't know.'*

The sun was beginning to sink, tinging the sky with delicate pink to the west. He called to Reddy and headed toward his apartment for another night of bachelorhood. A man and his cat.

Chapter Twelve

Sammy

Reddy trotted alongside Rommey as they approached the office on the cool and bright morning. In the distance, Rommey noticed a shady looking character pacing near the front steps of his office building with his hoodie pulled up and his hands hanging in the front pocket. From a half a block away, Rommey saw the patent attorney approach the stoop, only to be solicited by the well-muscled stranger. The attorney shook his head "no" to some inaudible question and proceeded up the stairs to the front door.

Once the attorney was inside, the guy cast about for his next victim and fixed his eyes on Rommey. *Great. Looks like an interaction is going to be unavoidable.* Rommey didn't look forward to being accosted first thing in the morning but he prepared himself to brush off the panhandler, hoping he wasn't the aggressive type.

Before Rommey reached the steps, the guy jammed his hands deeper into the pocket of his gray hoodie and stepped forward. "Excuse me. Are you Rommey Clipper?"

"Who's asking?"

"Um, I'm Sammy. I'm looking for...um, an editor?" The question in his voice indicated he wasn't sure what he was asking.

Rommey stopped and said, "That's me."

"Great, I've been waiting for you. I mean, I hate to jump on you first thing in the morning, but I can't wait any longer," Sammy said.

"Why don't you come up and we can talk about...well, whatever you came here for."

"Sure. Thanks." They turned and climbed the stairs together, with Reddy bounding up the steps in the lead. Inside, they passed the mafia guy in the hallway, who gave them a questioning look, maybe wondering if Rommey was hiring his own bodyguards now.

"Let me get the door open and some lights turned on. I'll just be a second. Make yourself comfortable." The man stood nervously, head down, with his hands together in front of him. Rommey returned from the back of the office with two mugs. "Coffee? It'll be ready in a few minutes."

"No thanks. I'm too jittery already," said Sammy.

"Well, have a seat them." Rommey joined him as they moved toward the sofa. "So why do you need an editor?"

"I have to be straight with you. I recently been released from jail." Sammy grimaced waiting for Rommey's reaction."

"I see. Go on."

"I didn't do what they said. I could never do that to a girl!" He squeezed his eyes closed with the pain of the thought of it. When he opened them, they beseeched Rommey to believe him. Even though I didn't do it, jail messed me up, just the same. Maybe even worse since I know I didn't deserve to go through all that."

"I can see how it would be especially difficult to deal with the injustice of being falsely jailed."

"You mean you believe me? Just like that? You don't need to see my release papers?"

"You seem like a straightforward guy to me. Besides, I don't think you would have found your way to me otherwise."

"That's cool. I figured I would be a suspect, you know, for the rest of my life. It's encouraging to think that maybe people will not hold jail time against me."

"So what bring you to my office?" Rommey asked.

"I'm not sure, to be honest. I heard you can help me. In fact, the message I keep seeing everywhere is 'Rommey Clipper can help you', so I came to see how that would work. I guess you could say I'm kind of shell shocked from being inside. How can you help me with that? Are you a counselor or something?"

"It's not counseling, but I help people forget by removing memories."

"Really? You could wipe these dreadful experiences from my mind? How about from my dreams? Can you keep me from dreaming I'm still inside so I can get some fu..., sorry, some sleep?"

"Once memories are gone, you won't dream about them anymore. So what do you want to forget?"

"A lot of things. Prison is a terrible place. Geez, that's a stupid thing to say. I'm sure you know prison sucks, but I don't think you can truly know the depth of darkness until you've been there. It doesn't rehab you. It makes you a much worse person than you ever were before going in. I want to forget the things I learned there. Things a person should never know. So many things…" he trailed off.

68

Without Sammy's notice, Reddy had situated himself in his lap and was being stroked.

"I understand. I can help you." Rommey said.

"I also want to let go of the anger about the wasted chunk of my life. I spent three years in the can before DNA evidence found the real shithead – oh sorry. I'm working on cleaning up my language. Yet another unwelcome souvenir of prison. Anyway, the guy who did this ruined two lives—hers and mine—maybe more. I mean that poor girl's family… I'm pissed about the wasted of a chunk of my life as much as anything. Can you remove both of those?

"I can. It's all related so it should be simple."

"How much does this cost? I should have asked sooner." He became rigid with anticipation of an answer he couldn't bear.

"There is a cost…"

"Oh man, I was afraid of that." Defeat weighed down his body, slumping his posture. "That's okay then. I'm sure I can't afford it. Now right now anyway. I haven't found a job yet, and…" He slid Reddy out of this lap and started to rise.

"Wait. Sammy. You didn't let me finish. It's not what you think." Sammy looked back. Tentative hope lurked in his eyes. "You just have to give me a memory. A good one."

"A cynical chuckle escaped Sammy's chest. "What if I don't have one?"

"You can pledge a future one."

"How do I know what's going to happen in the future?" he asked, confusion contorting his face.

"You don't. You don't get to choose a future memory. It will just be taken." Rommey answered.

Sammy thought in silence for a moment before saying, "I've lost too much of my present. I'm not giving up any chance for goodness in my future. I'll sacrifice an old memory." Then a smile lit his face, "I have the perfect one. The day my sentence was overturned. It was joyous, but I won't even need that memory when all the rest is gone, will I?"

"Clever choice. And since your conviction was overturned, your record will be scrubbed clean. I will just give you a suggestion of where you were during those three years in case anyone asks. What do you want to have been doing during those years?"

"I want to have been working, getting married, saving for a house - the usual stuff. That's what I mean about the missing chunk of my life. Anyway, for this we need something no one can check, I guess, don't we. Maybe I was backpacking through Europe. No, I've got it. Let's say I was working on a fishing boat in Alaska. No one will check, and I have no desire to be a fisherman, so I'll never have to look like I have that kind of experience."

"Perfect. I'll remind you of that after the unwanted memories are gone. Now, I have a document for you to read so you know exactly what you're agreeing to. Then we can start if you decide to proceed."

"Let's do this!" Sammy rubbed his hands together in anticipation.

Rommey presented Sammy with the Acknowledgment, which he read with intensity, then quickly signed. He then wrung his hands, unsure of what to do next. As Rommey set up the vessel, Sammy sat stiffly upright, obviously on edge.

As Rommey took his seat across from Sammy he said, "Okay Sammy, just relax and begin wherever you like. But please just tell me about the things you want to forget."

"Got it."

Even before Sammy started talking Rommey could see the mist beginning to rise from his short-cropped hair in anticipation of its exit, anxious to push out the vile memories.

"When I was arrested at the garage where I was working, I was shocked and confused. But since I knew I hadn't done anything wrong, I figured it would work itself out. The first blow was being held without bail. As a violent offender, bail wasn't an option. From the beginning, I was assumed to be guilty. That old line about innocent until proven guilty is a crock of, well you know.

When it came to the trial, the court-appointed lawyer they provided told me to plead guilty to get a reduced sentence. I was shocked. Why would I plead guilty to something I didn't do? It was unthinkable! The attorney was nonchalant and said, 'Suit yourself. It's your choice.' He almost had me convinced to plead guilty. They said the girl picked me out of a line-up. I found out later that wasn't true. The guy wore a mask and it was dark. God! That poor girl." He squeezed his eyes closed at the thought of the horror she must have gone through.

"I can't imagine the terror she felt. Well, yeah, I can, now that I've been preyed upon. Only mine wasn't minutes or even hours of horror. It was three long years of it. Not that I'm trying to say what happened to her wasn't horrible. It was. Unforgivable. But being suspicious, on guard, expecting the worse to happen at any minute for years on end takes a different kind of toll on your mind. You learn to see the worst of humanity, the depravity. It makes you jumpy. You never really sleep. And I'm not a big guy, so I had to stake my territory or be crushed. So much violence." Sammy stopped to steady his breathing. After a moment, he continued. "It all works together to strip you down. It removes your humanity. You are reduced to your animal core – scared and violent. And the boredom..." He stopped again, shaking his head. "That alone will make you lose your mind."

While he spoke, an ugly rainbow of hurt and regret poured from Sammy – red anger, and grey humiliation, intertwined with black fear, and brown regret. The orange of revenge mixed with the grayish green of violence and white of sorrow, ridding his body and mind of destructive memories.

"Then when it's over, they dump you back into the so-called 'real world' where people expect you to act like none of it happened. If someone bumps into you, you're supposed to say 'sorry', smile, and go on your way, not bow up and threaten to the break the guy's neck before he breaks yours. They expect you to look people in the eye when you talk to them. Doing that inside will get you a shiv between the ribs, or worse." Sammy continued to detail the degradation and violence he suffered daily for a crime he didn't commit. It seemed that every moment was another chance to be beaten, raped, or killed. Life was cheap and dispensable.

"Inside, you quickly learn to keep all emotions to yourself, except hostility, that is. So how and I supposed to ever have friends, or be able to interact with my family, much less have a relationship with a woman when I'm suspicious, withdrawn, and cynical of any expression of affection?"

"All those destructive memories are leaving you even you as relate them to me, Sammy. You should be feeling lighter and less tortured already." Rommey could see the tension easing from his body, as the vapors left him. He was winding down now, and the memories he told pulled out related memories along with them.

"Is there anything else you want to tell me?" Rommey asked.

Sammy's mind was clearing, and he was finally relaxed. "I just want to leave the anger about the wasted years behind and to get on with what's left of my life."

"I think we've got that covered. You just rest a minute and I'll be right back."

"Okay," Sammy mumbled from behind closed eyes.

Rommey went to put on the tea. While it was heating, he consulted his list of contacts and wrote down a name and number before returning to Sammy's side.

"Hey Sammy," he called softly. Sammy struggled to open his eyes. "Hey, buddy. How ya feeling?"

Sammy mumbled, "Okay."

"Before we finish, I want to give you this." He handed Sammy a slip of paper. "I'm editing a book for a guy who owns a car dealership. Here are his name and number. He's always looking for reliable help. I'll give him a call and tell him to expect you. Those last three years you spent fishing in Alaska will give you the perseverance to succeed."

"Thanks, man."

"No problem. Now let me get you some tea."

Chapter Thirteen

Kylie

Reddy was lying on the back of the black-brown sofa washing his face while soaking in the morning sun. When the door opened, he took one look at the visitor and retreated to a safe spot underneath the couch. Rommey strolled out of his office, coffee cup in hand, to greet the finely dressed blonde woman who had entered. The plum Prada bag over her forearm perfectly matched her Ann Taylor ensemble.

"Good morning," Rommey said.

"Are you Rommey Clipper?"

Reddy could be heard faintly growling. "Yes, that's right. May I help you?" He cast a questioning glance under the sofa at Reddy.

"My name is Kylie Banner. I think I'm supposed to see you."

"Oh? Are you a writer?" he asked, knowing full well she wasn't.

"Uh, no. I don't work." She blinked slowly. "It's just that wherever I'm stewing about a problem, your name comes to mind. It's weird."

"And then you found my card?"

"Yes, how did you know?" Kylie asked, eyes wide.

"I've seen it happen before. So, something is bothering you? Would you like to tell me about it?"

"For some reason, I would. I have a problem you see." She paused as if Rommey should know what she was talking about.

"And that problem is…?"

"I think, um, I think it would be best for me if I forgot someone."

"Did he or she hurt you?" There was no answer, just a pensive expression. "Did you hurt them?" he asked tilting his head and raising his brows.

"Well, it sounds kind of petty when I say it out loud." She looked like second thoughts were appearing now that she was here.

"It's okay. I hear lots of people's stories. You won't shock me."

"Well, it's just that someone I know has this perfect life. She gets all the breaks. Everything comes so easy to her." A slight whine had crept into her voice.

"You're jealous."

"No! I'm not jealous. I'm…I'm sad about the unfairness. Yes, that's it! She makes me sad," she ended, obviously proud of her wordsmithing.

"You resent her life, then?" Rommey asked.

"Yes. I mean, I don't think she shouldn't have it. I just think I should have it too," replied the petulant young woman. I don't even know why I'm telling you this. Are you a shrink or something?"

"No, I'm an editor." Kylie looked confused. Rather than letting her try to work through her question, Rommey decided it would be more expedient just to explain it to her. "I edit writers' works, but I also help people get rid of memories that bother them."

"You do? There are people who do that?" She crossed her right arm over her narrow waist and rested her hand on her left wrist which still dangled the tidy Prada handbag.

"A few," Rommey answered.

She placed her right hand on her hip. "I didn't even know that service was available! That's fantastic. That is what I want then. Do you have a menu of services you provide…like at the spa? I want to see what all of my options are."

"That's it really. Written work edited. Memories removed. That's the extent of the 'services' offered here."

"I just want to make sure I get all the goodies. Like the luxury package." She smiled brightly.

Rommey was growing weary of this professional shopper. "Again it's just editing writing or memories. Take it or leave it."

"Well, you don't have to get snippy. I was just asking." Her expression had gone from excited to annoyed in an instant. Rommey ran his hand through this hair while he composed himself in a more accommodating demeanor.

"I'm sorry, Ms. Banner. You were saying about your friend?"

"Oh, she's not my friend. Not really anyway. I mean I was nice to her face, but we weren't close, even before she hit it big." Kylie's pout had disappeared as quickly as it had come now that she was talking about her issue again.

"Would I know this person? Is she a public figure?"

"I'm sure you'd recognize her name. She's a famous singer-songwriter. Ow! See how even saying that makes my stomach hurt? Anyway, her debut album spent 157 weeks on the charts. One hundred and fifty-seven! – the longest period in history! Who does that? And she was sixteen. And now she's worth over a quarter of billion dollars. That's billion with a 'B'! And a B like in Banner – the person who *should* be in her shoes." Kylie was exhausted from relating all the things that plagued her. She sighed heavily with exasperation and headed for the nearest seat.

Rommey followed her to the couch and said quietly, "I can't remove her fame if that's what you're after."

"That's too bad," she paused. "Then can you make it so I don't remember I ever knew her? That would help."

"You think that would make you feel better?" asked Rommey.

"Oh, much! I only feel a little bit of jeal...um, sadness about other rich and famous people that I don't know. But with 'T', as we shall call her, I feel like I was *this* close to fame and fortune, but instead, I just missed it somehow."

"You know you'll still see her in the news, right?"

"Well, I won't have to remember that I knew her."

"You don't think her success has to do with her creativity, talent, and hard work then?"

"Well, maybe a little," she reluctantly acknowledged. "But it couldn't carry her as far as she's gone. It must be mostly luck, and luck could have just as easily have fallen on me," she pouted again.

"You know some people have truly terrible things befall them. Bad luck, tragedy, violence, and still they struggle and persevere." There was an uncomprehending cock of her head. He tried again, "You look like you are doing well in life."

"Thank you," she responded completely missing Rommey's meaning. "Now once you remove my knowledge of Miss Swift, I mean 'T', I'll be much happier. Shall we begin?" she asked brightly, brushing past Rommey as she headed toward his office.

"There is a cost," said Rommey to her back.

"Whatever it is I'll pay it," she said with a dismissive wave of the hand, without turning around.

"It's not like that."

Kylie stopped and turned toward Rommey. "What then? I thought you said there was a price. Money is no object."

"No, I said there is a cost," he said as he closed the gap between them. "The cost is either a memory you cherish or a future good memory. The good thing will still happen, but you won't remember it. It's on the agreement I need for you to read."

"Paperwork, yuck!" she lamented as she followed him into his office.

Rommey slid around behind his desk and pulled out the Acknowledgment and handed it to Kylie.

"Ooo! It has my name engraved on it already! That's so posh!"

Rommey raised his eyebrows and exhaled. This was not the usual kind of help he gave, but maybe a light one was due after hearing the tragedy of Sammy's tale.

After signing the parchment without reading most of it, Kylie nestled into her seat with her head tilted back, closed her eyes, and waited as if she was preparing for a facial.

"Kylie, what kind of memory are you going to forfeit?"

"Hmm?" she asked without opening her eyes.

"A memory. Item five of the Acknowledgment. You must either forfeit a happy old memory of your choice, or a future one of our choosing. What's it going to be?"

"Who cares about the past. Take one of those. I'm all about the future."

"You'll have to specify which one before we can start."

"Oh, take the one where I got the fluffy white puppy for my birthday. I was pretty excited at the time, but who cares about that now. I don't even remember his name. Or was it a girl? Anyway, take that one."

"10-4," Rommey said coldly.

"Now do I just tell you my story? Okay. It all began-
"

"Please hold just a moment while I prepare." He went ahead and put the teapot on. This wasn't going to take long. Then taking a seat across from her, he said, "Okay, you may begin."

"It all started in the eighth grade when she appeared at Hendersonville High School. Her family moved there just so her family could be close to Nashville – and to ruin my life, apparently. She had already been taking acting and singing lessons by that point. Hmm. I just realized that if she was really all that talented, she wouldn't have needed all those lessons, now would she?"

"I wouldn't know. Please continue," urged Rommey.

"Before long she was auditioning for the talent show. She didn't even care that we popular girls hadn't approved her yet! It was like she didn't even need our okay to put herself out there that like that. Crazy, I know. And kinda rude if you ask me."

"Appalling," Rommey said without conviction. Boredom and contempt wrestled for top billing on this drivel. A thin silver stream of average disappointment mingled with the dark green vapor of jealousy as it streamed toward the jug.

"Anyway, she didn't stay at my school but a couple of years, thankfully. After she left, things got back to normal, with my friends and me on top, as it should have been all along. But even after that, I still couldn't be free of her. She's on social media all the time. Just this morning, I saw…"

Rommey cut her off saying, "I think that about covers your memories of her, wouldn't you say?" The last of the green vapor was just entering the bottle.

"Well, yes, I guess." She seemed sad to lose her audience.

"You just sit tight. I have your tea almost ready."

"Tea? What kind?"

"Chamomile and honey," he said.

"Do you have any cookies? Gluten-free preferably. And maybe green tea, instead? Or kombucha? I love kombucha," she called after him.

"No, just chamomile."

"Oh, pooh!"

"I'm sure you'll survive," he mumbled, unconcerned whether she heard him or not.

Chapter Fourteen

Muriel

Reddy peeked out from under the sofa to make sure Kylie had left before resuming his bath in the sun patch. After walking around his office and staring out the window for a minute to shake off the slightly foul feeling she had left in her wake, Rommey returned to editing the novel he was working on. He had just gotten to a humorous bit where several elves were trying to feed a dragon without being bar-be-qued when he heard the outer door open. He feared Kylie had returned for some reason, but instead, he found a middle-aged woman, her dark hair pulled into a neat twist in the back, holding his card.

"Oh hello. I thought you might be someone else," Rommey said.

"I'm sorry to intrude. I can come back another time. Can I make an appointment?"

"Sure, but truly, I'm grateful it was not who I thought it might be." He smiled. "I'm Rommey. Are you here to see me?"

"I believe so, yes." She looked into his eyes but didn't say more.

"May I ask what it is about?"

"I don't know yet," she said matter-of-factly.

"And yet you want to make an appointment, even though you don't know what it's for?"

"That's right." She paused, seeming to wait for him to understand. "You see, I'm very spiritual."

"Okay…" said Rommey, hoping for more explanation.

"There are things we won't understand until the time is right," she replied.

"I see. Why *did* you come here today, Ms.…?"

"It's Muriel. I was called. Or it's more like I was *shown* here, I guess you would say. I felt drawn to your address. Doover Street. Did you notice it contains the words 'do-over'?"

"The idea of a do-over attracted you here?"

"Maybe that's it. A do-over, yes, that *must* be it," she added with confidence.

"What would you like to do over?" asked Rommey.

"Well, …it's shameful. I'm too ashamed of myself to say it."

"What if I told you I might be able to help you with it, whatever the shameful thing is?"

"Unless you can turn back time, that's not possible," she confided.

"No, I can't do that, but I might be able to help by working on the memory of whatever it was," offered Rommey.

"You could?" She thought deeply for a moment, then asked, "Would that be right?"

"Only you can answer that."

"If I wanted to stop remembering something, could you help me with that?"

"Yes," he answered.

"How would it work?" Muriel listened critically as Rommey explained the procedure.

"I'm not sure if that is ethical," Muriel furrowed her brow.

"Why don't you tell me briefly what happened and maybe I can help you decide."

"After considering the idea for a minute, she and Rommey moved to the sofa for a seat. Reddy made himself comfortable next to Muriel, tucking his paws under his chest and purring quietly.

"I saw a man being beaten, and I did nothing to stop it. I feel just sick about my cowardice. I can't get the pictures out of my head. Why didn't I help? Why didn't I try?" she nearly begged for an answer she had never been able to find.

"Maybe because it wasn't safe to get in the middle of men fighting? That doesn't sound cowardly. It sounds horrible, but also understandable."

"I did call 911—I was looking down on the scene from my apartment—but it was a while before the ambulance and police arrived. Once I was sure the gang had left, I wanted to go down to be with him, but I was too scared they would return. I should have tried to stop it in the first place." Muriel covered her face with her hands, hiding her tears.

"Do you honestly think you could have broken it up? It sounds like it was several men against one."

"It was," Muriel admitted. Sadness constricted her voice.

"I don't think you should feel guilty, but if you'd like for me to remove the traumatic images, I can do that."

Muriel was still unsure. "I think I need to think about it more now that I know I have this option. Maybe living with the memories is the price I must pay for my inaction. Maybe it's my penance. Remembrance as penance."

"It doesn't seem to be of any benefit. You did what you could in a terrible situation. We owe ourselves the gift of forgiveness." Rommey added.

"Maybe," she said, obviously considering his words. "And I *was* drawn here. There has to be a reason for that."

"How about I give you some time to think about it. I was just about to make some coffee. Would you like a cup?"

"Do you have tea? I never learned to drink coffee," said Muriel.

"Is chamomile okay?"

"Oh, yes. That's one of my favorites. Thank you."

While Rommey busied himself making tea, he heard Muriel discussing her plight with Reddy as he purred along in response to her stroking. When Rommey returned with two cups, her eyes were clear with her decision.

"I'd like to go ahead with the procedure," she said with confidence.

"I'm glad to hear that. It sounds like you have suffered enough. Those men victimized more than just the man they assaulted. I'm sorry you had to go through that. You just enjoy your tea, and Reddy will keep you company while I set up."

"Certainly," she smiled, relief softening her face.

This is what an Editor should be doing, not placating the Kylies of the world. Helping Muriel was just the perfect antidote to Kylie.

Chapter Fifteen

Terrance and Jake

Rommey wasn't surprised to see Terrance standing in his reception area. He had met him briefly at the coffee shop when Terrance had somehow managed to work the story of his life's disappointment into their introductory conversation. Thirty-something Terrance told Rommey that he was a starting pitcher in high school who had been scouted by a major league farm team. It hadn't worked out, and his life was ruined.

Rommey had heard bits of this story before, only in the previous version, he was being scouted by the University of Georgia. It seemed the story was growing along with Terrance's disenchantment with life.

"Can I help you?" Rommey asked Terrance.

"Hey, you're that guy from the coffee shop. I found your card in my pocket," Terrance looked slightly confused.

"Oh yeah?"

"Yeah. It seems like …I think you are supposed to help me with a problem."

"What problem is that?" Rommey asked.

"Your card says, 'because forgetting is impossible'. What does that mean?"

"It means that people can decide to forgive someone, but the memory of the incident stays with them. For some people, continuing to remember is a problem."

"Remembering is a problem," Terrance mutter to himself. "I have a problem like that. Do you help people deal with troublesome memories?

"I do," answered Rommey.

"Huh. No kidding."

"Yep, no kidding."

"I can't stop thinking about what might have been. Can you help me forget about that? I have all these regrets, ya know? It's driving me crazy."

"Maybe you need a counselor, not an editor." His distaste for Terrance was growing as they talked.

"I don't need no shrink." Terrance's tone was defensive. "I just don't want to remember what I almost had. Do you have some kind of treatment or procedure for that?"

"I can help you if you want a memory gone. Do you think that will help, though?"

"I do," answered Terrance. "I was on my way to being a famous baseball player, but I worked too hard and messed up my shoulder. It's never been right since."

"You don't think maybe lack of conditioning affected that? Or that you could have moved on to different pursuits when that didn't work out?"

"No man. My whole future was shot."

"I see." Yielding to his duty to help anyone who asked, Rommey agreed to edit his memory to remove *what almost was* so Terrance could get on with his life.

During the session, a small wisp of the silvery gray mist of disappointment escaped from Terrance. Less than fifteen minutes later, Terrance had drunk his tea and was on his way.

Well, that sort of felt like a waste of time, but it brings me one clip closer to earning my life back, so I'll take it.

Rommey's afternoon appointment wasn't due for a few hours so he settled down behind his computer and returned to editing the fantasy tome. He was having trouble keeping up with which creature had which magical power and which weakness. His confusion wasn't helped by the fact that the names all had too many vowels and apostrophes like O'El and A'Khit. They didn't exactly roll off the tongue or stick in the memory. He needed a playbill to keep everyone straight. *That's it! I'll suggest the author include a glossary of names and attributes with a pronunciation guide. I'll be a hero to the readers, and they won't even know it.*

At two p.m. on the nose, Jake Gipson entered Rommey's office for his appointment.

"Hey, Jake. Right on time, I see."

"Yes sir," he said. Rommey couldn't say what it was, but Jake looked troubled somehow. *Maybe he's was just anxious about having his work reviewed.*

"Come on into my office and let's see what you have." Rommey took his desk chair, while Jake tried to sit comfortably in the guest chair across the desk that looked absurdly too small under his bulk. "So were you able to write about non-battle parts of your story like we talked about last time?"

Jake's jaw tightened visibly. "I tried. I thought about what I wanted to say non-stop, but every time I started to write something down, it didn't sound right. I couldn't put it into words."

"Sometimes it helps if you don't try to write in chronological order. Just write what is most present and pressing on your mind. It doesn't even have to be whole sentences. Often once you get started, thoughts come more easily. The sentences and sections can be placed in order later," Rommey offered.

"It doesn't matter where I start, it doesn't come out right. Maybe this is a stupid idea. Why did I even think I could write a book?" Anger mixed with frustration was seeping out in his words and posture. His breath quickened as he flexed his hands into large fists.

Wanting to help Jake with his anguish, Rommey suggested, "Would it be easier if you forgot the whole incident?"

Before the words were out of Rommey's mouth, Jake answered with an empathic "NO! I'll never forget it. That would mean I would have to forget my brothers and I'd *never* do that. It would dishonor us all." He stared hard at Rommey for the offense of such a suggestion.

"I'm sorry. I didn't mean to be disrespectful. I apologize," said Rommey.

Jake's scowl softened and Rommey saw the tension in his jaw ease slightly. Then he continued more quietly, "It's my job to remember, to honor my brothers, to always carry them with me. Just like they would do if I was killed instead of them. I think that's the thing we dread the most, you know?"

"What's that?"

"I mean after leaving behind family and friends who depend on us, the hardest thing to face is the idea of being forgotten. We know our unit will never forget us, just as I'll never forget them regardless of whether it causes me pain every single day." Jack paused and was silent for a moment as his grimace softened into a smile. "Besides, we had a lot of fun, too." He chuckled slightly at the memories. "The guys in your units are closer than family. They are the only ones who know what you've been through."

"So I understand. I never served," said Rommey.

"Yeah, having a reasonable chance of dying every day – well, you learn to make the best of the time you have, and you get real close with the people who are going through it with you. Real close." He smiled again. "Man, I miss those dipshits," he finished, chuckling. "Mind you, if anyone else called them dipshits, they'd have me to contend with. I'd take them out!" He pointed his large finger in Rommey's direction, as he smiled. His previous misstep was forgiven that quickly.

"Understood," Rommey replied with a sympathetic smile. "What do you say we change to talking about the arch of the story instead of the details?" Seeing the confusion on Jake's face, he added, "Where the story begins and ends – a rough idea of the events you want to include."

"Okay, it should start with the patrol that day."

"That's good. We can work in the relationship between you guys, how you met, some things you had been through together, as the story progresses. We might even do some flashbacks. Sorry, I'm getting ahead of myself. Don't worry about putting it together at this point. Like I said before, you can write in any order and assemble it later. We can work all that out. Let's just try to get the parts outlined.

"It helps me to see that you are honestly interested in the story. I start to try to write, then I get overwhelmed. Then I wonder if anyone is going to want to read it. Then I think that if they do read it, what if they think it's crap?"

"That is more common than you might think for writers."

"But when we talk about it, you take it seriously, like it could be a book. A real book," said Jake. "I want to write about what happened, tell how hard and how well we worked together. I want to memorialize the guys we lost."

"Now we're getting there," said Rommey. "Keep talking."

Chapter Sixteen

Anna

Rommey and Reddy returned from lunch to find a mouse of a woman sitting on the floor outside the door. She was not much more than a girl, at least Rommey thought she was a girl, but dressed in androgynous, loose-fitting jeans and sweatshirt with roughly cropped hair, it was hard to be sure.

"Hey, kitty," she said as she saw Reddy approach.

"His name is Reddy. Are you waiting for him?" Rommey asked, smiling.

As she unfolded herself to her full five-foot-two-inch height, she said, "I think I'm here to see you. If you are the editor, that is."

"Yes, I'm Rommey," he said extending his hand.

"I'm Anna," she said as she offered her small hand to meet his.

"What can I do for you?" He asked.

"This is going to sound weird," she grimaced. "I had a dream, well several really, saying that you could help me. I've prayed about it for so long and never gotten an answer. Or maybe this is the answer from heaven. I don't know. I'm all mixed up. I get confused and I don't understand things that I know sometimes. That doesn't even make sense, does it? I have an...um, understanding... or something." She exhaled heavily with frustration at her inability to explain. "It's just that I see things that others don't sometimes. I think it's from spending so much time alone, lost in my own thoughts. I think about things that other people don't seem to, like how the world would be if everyone was honest. There be no stealing, but there'd also be no lock companies, or locksmiths, or PINs, or cameras everywhere. It would put a lot of people out of work. That's something people don't think about."

Rommey was chuckling as he unlocked the door. Anna followed him inside still chattering on.

"And I think about how many creatures make a living from a tree —all the caterpillars, birds, squirrels, and deer to eat the acorns, and fungus to break down the old leaves and recycle them into fertilizer for the tree. I'm sorry, I'm babbling. It's because I'm nervous."

"You're an engaging person, Anna. Is there something I can help you with?" Rommey asked.

"Well, like I was saying, I hear things others don't."

"Okaaay…," he encouraged her on. He tucked his hands in his pockets as they stopped in the middle of the reception area.

"And what I keep hearing is you. Your name."

She is definitely in need of a clip, it's just a question of for what. "My name?"

"Yes. Like 'See Rommey Clipper to set you free.' I don't know what that means, but I know it's important."

"People usually receive that kind of message because something is bothering them, like a memory that is especially painful or distressing."

"Oh." She grew quiet and looked down at her clasped hands, shifting her weight as she thought. Then she looked up at Rommey as tears welled in her eyes. Her face then hardened as she sniffed and roughly wiped away the unspilled tears. Curiosity took over and she said, "Let's say for a minute a person did have especially painful or distressing memories, like you say. What do you do?"

"Well, I edit them. I'm an editor, you see?" He pointed toward the writing on the door.

"I thought an editor published books and wrote magazines," Anna said.

"I do work with written documents, yes, but I also edit memories." He paused a minute to let the information settle in her mind. "Is that something of interest to you?"

"Maybe," she paused, skepticism showing on her face. "For real, though? How does it work? Does it hurt? How much does it cost? Is this for real or a scam, 'cause I'm not falling for a scam." Her face hardened again.

"Let's have a seat and I'll try to answer your questions," Rommey offered, then motioned her toward the couch.

"Where is the rest of your furniture?" Anna looked around as if it might be hiding in a corner somewhere.

"The sofa and my office furniture are all I have. It came with the office and I'm not much for shopping or decorating, I'm afraid."

"It's kind of dismal in here," she said, looking sorry that she had said it, or maybe just sorry for him. Reddy had centered himself in a patch of sun on one of the cushions and stretched out to his full length, his white belly exposed. "But Reddy sure seems fine with the sofa as it is. He's such a handsome fella."

Reddy licked one white paw, luxuriating in the compliment.

"How did you know he's a boy?"

"Oh, I assumed. Most orange tabbies are male. It's a sex-linked gene in cats."

Rommey was becoming charmed by her off-beat and wide-ranging knowledge. "I thought you said you didn't know things. It sounds like you know a lot of things and have a clever mind."

"No, I said I didn't understand some things I know. That's different. It's like I see another side of things that others don't. Sometimes even *I* don't understand it. It's hard to explain." Seated on the couch next to Reddy, her hand instinctively reached over to smooth the silky fur from his ears down his spine. He readily gave in to the strokes and left his ablutions until later.

"Let me see if I can remember your questions. First, Yes, I can remove memories. Second, how does it work? After some preliminary things, you tell me your memory, and I take them away. Does it hurt? Only as much as recalling the memory. The good news is you'll never have to think about it again." Then he explained the process of removing the memory and the sacrifice of good memory in return for the removal of the bad ones.

"What if I've tried so hard to forget all the badness, that I don't remember to tell you all of it. But then I remember something else about it later? Am I stuck with those memories then?"

"All the related memories should come out together. They are pretty interwoven, so it isn't usually a problem," he answered.

"I can't believe we're talking about this like it's an everyday kind of thing." She looked troubled as she considered Rommey's explanations. "I don't know if I want to remember all that," she said quietly.

"That's your choice. You can choose not to proceed anytime until we actually start. You are welcome to think about it as long as you like. You won't be able to discuss it with anyone, but you can come back to my office at any time. There will always be an editor here, during office hours, that is." Rommey smiled. He wanted to keep talking with her and getting to know her and her quirky, fascinating thought process. *It's too bad she won't remember me if she chooses to be clipped.*

Anna bit her lip and stroked Reddy as she thought. "I don't know. I almost feel like I can trust you, but it's hard. I'll admit it. You did say this isn't a scam, right?"

"If it was a scam, would I admit it?" he asked, bemused. "I can't tell you if it's right for you. I can only answer any questions you have."

With reticence, Anna replied, "I think I need to think about it. Aren't you going to ask me about my memories?"

"They are really none of my business."

"But don't you need to know what you're after in there?" She asked, pointing to her head.

"You'll tell me if you decide to have them edited."

"So, I won't remember any of it afterward?"

"Nope."

"Will I remember you?"

"Nope."

She sat quietly; her mouth pressed into a firm line as she thought. "I think I need to think about it."

"That's fine. You know where to find me, and Reddy," he smiled, "if you decide to, you know, be edited."

"Alright, Mr. Clipper. I'll be thinking," she vowed, tapping her temple. And before his eyes, as she left, he saw her withdraw again into the small, unnoticeable creature who he had found sitting by his door.

Chapter Seventeen

Jacob

Whew, I'm beat, thought Rommey. *I can't even focus on my screen anymore and there is a fire between my shoulder blades from reading for so long. I think I'll stop by The Hooch on the way home for a beer. It would be nice to be around some people for a while even if I don't know them. I just need to feel some life and conversation around me.*

"You won't mind hanging out here for a while, will you Reddy?" Reddy didn't even twitch a whisker at the mention of his name. He was deeply into his fifth or sixth nap of the day.

It felt good to be up moving around as Rommey walked the few blocks to The Hooch Brewery. The warmth and convivial murmurs welcomed him as he entered. Heading to the bar, he spotted Jacob, the birdman from the park, and took the stool next to him.

"Hey, it's Jacob, right?"

"Oh hey, yeah. Um, I'm sorry I don't remember your name. We talked in the park…"

"Yeah, it's Rommey," he said, extending his hand.

Taking it, Jacob said, "Oh that's right. How's your buddy, Reddy?"

"Good, snoozing on his favorite sofa at the office. I didn't want to wake him. He needs his beauty rest." They both chuckled.

The TV above the bar was tuned to the news. The news caster said, "Ankara reports today more clashes between the Turks and Kurds in northern Turkey, as an offensive to push the Kurds over the border into Syria increases in intensity. U.S. forces are seeking to establish a demilitarized zone- "

After watching for a couple of minutes, Jacob said, "The middle east will never be at peace. They've been fighting as long as tribes have existed."

"I've wondered if humans can ever mind their own business and be happy with what they have," said Rommey

"Not as long as they have memories."

Intrigued, Rommey asked, "Oh? How so?"

"Think about it. Every retaliation spawns a reaction that feeds the next violent response. After a while, no one remembers the original act, but the hatred is woven into their DNA," said Jacob.

"Interesting you should say that. I've thought about this a good bit. For example, what if Al Qaeda fighters could forget their radicalization? Or what if the Hutus could forget their slaughter at the hands of the Tutsis? And in America, no one has owned slaves for 150 years, but there is still so much animosity, hatred, racial sensitivity that lingers and is now ingrained in our society. What if the Scottish and English, or the Jews and their oppressors could be washed of all prejudices and old pain and insults, broken hearts and fury, atrocities, and disdain? Humanity could start with a clean slate.

"Too bad that isn't possible. On the other hand, don't you think that humans, even without old grievances and prejudices, would just do it all over again – take advantage of the weaker tribe starting the whole cycle of hatred all

97

over again? 'Those who forget history are doomed to repeat it' and all like that," said Jacob.

"But so many old grievances have piled up over the centuries. Surely we'd be better off starting fresh."

Jacob thought about this scenario for a moment with his forearms resting on the bar. "If only. Even if it could be done for individual people, what a change that could make in a life."

"Like for people to become 'un-tortured' by memories of abuse, for example?" asked Rommey.

"Yeah that, but also remembering terrible things they had done if they didn't mean to do them." Jacob's face was clouding, growing morose as the conversation continued.

"It could change a life."

"Yeah, if only," repeated Jacob.

Rommey sensed something was dogging Jacob, but it was not his place to ask. Nor was it his job to suggest an edit. If an edit was needed, Jacob would come to him when it was time. For now, it was nice to enjoy a beer and some conversation like a normal person.

Chapter Eighteen

Eric

Eric came to Rommey's office in the usual way, and like many of his memory clients, Eric's trouble had worn itself into his face and body.

Eric's request was an unusual one though: he wanted to forget this wife. A wife that he adored.

After they had talked about the basics for a few minutes, Rommey asked, "Do you have kids? We can't do this if you have kids. We can't have you suddenly not remembering their mother."

"No, we…," the rest was lost in anguished tears. When Eric had somewhat composed himself, he continued. "No kids. I'm not sure I can do this. So, I won't remember her at all?"

"Look, maybe you're not ready for this," suggested Rommey. "Or maybe it's not what you want to do at all. There's no rush. We can do it whenever you are ready, or not at all if that's what you decide."

"I'm sure. And here's why. I've been weeping for four years. I can't bear the pain of it any longer. I can't eat. I can't sleep. A guy who is crying in the bathroom at work— again— because he overheard someone talking about what to get his wife for her birthday, is not the kind of guy most people want to work with. I've lost another job.

"I've been living on our savings." The word *our* choked him up again. "Anyway, I'm running out of money. I have to find a way to get past it. Booze didn't dull the anguish. Religion, grief therapy— none of it made any difference. So I beg you, take all of the beautiful moments of our brief... so brief," here he lost his voice for a moment, "time together and put them somewhere—I don't know—somewhere else so I can have a chance to live out my life. Otherwise, I'm going to finish it all off much earlier than god, or whoever, intended."

Rommey started to speak, but Eric continued.

"Don't think I haven't thought about that option, I've been close several times, but then I keep hearing your name. 'Rommey Clipper can help', it says. At first, I thought it was on TV, but when I looked up, it was a pizza commercial. Then I thought I heard someone say 'There's Rommey Clipper', but when I turned around no one was there. I dreamed it, too. Then I found your card in my pocket. I didn't think I needed an editor, but now I understand. You do a very different kind of editing. Anyway, can you help me? Will you help me by editing my memory?"

Rommey's heart went out to the haggard man, about his own age but looking much older. "Yes, of course."

Once Eric had reviewed the consent form, Rommey showed him to the chair and asked him to make himself comfortable so they could begin. "We usually start with choosing a good memory to forfeit, but since many of yours will pleasant ones, we can dispense with that step. Tell me about your wife."

Eric rested his head back against the chair, eyes closed in exhaustion. "Alee was...well, there was no one like her. She could light up the whole outdoors with her smile. There was such a sweetness about her. But she was strict, too. She could spot a disingenuous person a mile away.

She'd politely listen to some guy's tall tale, then inform him 'that dog won't hunt'. Or she would say, 'he's crooked as a dog's hind leg'." Eric smiled now at the memory. "She has an unlimited number of those old southern phrases.

"We met in high school. It was instant with us. Once we met, I don't think we were ever apart for more than a few hours. We dated for the 3 years we were in high school and college together. We stupidly got married before we finished college, but somehow, we made it through. Married student's housing was the worst! But at least we were together."

Rommey saw his bony body sink farther into the chair as he relaxed in a haze of pleasant memories. Mist was rising from him now but was unlike any Rommey had ever seen. It was pink, the pink of true, pure love. That was not something most people wanted to forget.

"We took out loans for school and our parents helped, but, man, were we broke! I delivered pizzas at night and Alee worked in the Admission Office between classes. We finally graduated, moved to Atlanta for jobs, and continued to work like crazy. Things were a little easier than in college, but we were still working long hours to make it in our careers. But we were young. You can do that when you're young. Boundless energy, and all that, right?"

"Right," said Rommey quietly, not wanting to disturb Eric's flow of recollections.

"I first noticed that Alee was falling asleep at odd times—midmorning on the way to the park on a Saturday, or between getting home from work and having dinner. She always had such an easy time falling asleep, I just thought it was funny. I teased her about it. Oh god, I teased her about it! We didn't know yet." Anguish had returned to his voice.

The purple vapor of deep pain was now mixing with the pure pink, as Eric's story edged toward the reason for his heartache. "You couldn't have known," offered Rommey.

"Quick naps became longer and longer. Then the headaches came with increasing frequency. Those sometimes took whole days to relent. Finally, we decided maybe they were migraines, so we went to a doctor. Alee hated taking anything but the pain was so bad, she agreed to see what relief was available.

"Migraine meds did not help and had dreadful side effects. Then there were more tests. All those tests. All the waiting in ugly waiting rooms with idiotic TV's yammering on like watching a home fix-it show was going to teach me to fix the only thing that mattered. I don't fucking care how to install new fancier crown molding. I wanted to fix my wife's brain tumor before it killed her! Did they have a program for that? That's what I wanted to see!"

Angry red vapor joined the flow now.

"The first surgery was terrifying, but we were so hopeful. They got most of it without damaging any other brain function. After a tough recovery, we spent the best year of our life together. We drank champagne with pizza, visited every art museum within driving distance, invited friends to sumptuous dinners or burgers on the grill. We lived in joy...until we both noticed her right-side weakness. I'm sure she noticed it first but didn't say anything. Then it became obvious to me, too.

"A second surgery trimmed back the tumor to 'give her more time', they said. I'll never forget hearing those words. That was when we understood she wouldn't beat it. They could only take about half of it without also taking her sight, which I would have gladly accepted, but her brain stem was involved too. You can live without sight, but not without respiration.

"At that point, we admitted defeat and tried to spend the time we had left together in a way that left me with valuable memories. Ironic, isn't it that now I want to be free of what we worked so hard to create? But I can't bear it anymore." His body sagged further into its exhaustion.

Rommey listened quietly to Eric's quiet desperation.

"Anyway, you can see where this story goes. It was horrific as all her major systems began to fail. Muscle control, including swallowing for god's sake. She had a hard time with a milkshake. It's as if nothing enjoyable was allowed for my sweet Alee. My Emmalee. My sweetheart from sophomore year. My Emmalee Hudgens, my South Georgia peach."

Eric dissolved into tears of heartbreak and exhaustion. The dark purple mist resolved back to light shimmering pink as the last of Eric's cherished, tortuous memories flowed   silently   into   the   vessel.

As Eric drifted off into a peaceful sleep, at last, Rommey quietly rose the cap the vessel holding the sweet and painful memories. After making tea, he returned to find Eric snoring quietly. *How long had it been since he had slept peacefully?* Rommey wondered. *He had a love so great it broke his heart. What irony there was. I dream of the day I can have a love again and build a new life, but man, this gives me pause.* Rommey exhaled a long breath, then gently woke Eric for his tea.

"Eric, you're going to enjoy your move to a new city. Look for a job and move there. Oh, and you never want to go to your class reunion, do you?"

"No reunion. New city," Eric mumbled.

~~~~~~

It wasn't until after Eric left that it hit Rommey like a punch to the gut. Eric's Alee, his Emmalee Hudgens, was none other than Edward Widdlefish's unrequited love, Emma. This woman was so captivating that her loss had resulted in anguish for two men, resulting in the memory of her being extinguished from the one she loved, as well as, the one she didn't.

Chapter Nineteen

Anna

There was a clamor in the hallway as Rommey finished off the tuna sandwich he was sharing with Reddy. Anna was back, this time trailed by two men with two wingback chairs, one with a coffee table strapped to it. Dressed in loose-fitting jeans and an old-fashioned western cut men's shirt, her slight figure gave little clue as to her gender. A baseball cap over short-cropped hair completed the look that let her hide in plain sight.

The turquoise, brown, and cream chairs coordinated perfectly with the brown-black sofa making it completely plausible as a furniture color. The coffee table was unstrapped and placed between the sofa and chairs creating a respectable reception area.

"Hi Anna. What's all this?" Rommey asked.

She slipped the delivery guys a bill with thanks. "These are two chairs and a coffee table."

"I see that. But why?"

"Because this place is desolate looking. And after today I won't remember you, so I won't be able to fix it. I'm thanking you in advance," she replied as if her answer was obvious. "Are you sure I won't remember you?"

"Positive."

"Well, that's a shame, right there. I like to keep up with the good people in my life." She scooted one of the chairs over a few inches and stood back to inspect the arrangement.

As she wrestled the chairs into place, Rommey noticed a light clover-shaped birthmark near her wrist. *She carries her luck with her, but I guess there are two kinds of luck: good and bad. She wouldn't be here if her lot fell to the good side.*

"Do you like them?" She crossed her arms and stared critically at the furniture.

"Very much. What do I owe you for them?" Rommey said, reaching for his wallet and she would accept partial payment for now.

"Oh, nothing. They came from the thrift store. I thought you needed them. It's amazing what people throw out: furniture, books, animals, kids…" she trailed off.

"So, you've come back about your memories, I presume?" He asked.

She took a deep breath and turned her attention to him. "Yep, I've decided it's time. I've suffered enough." She grew quieter. The memories shut out the light that moments ago was pouring from this girl. When she wasn't thinking of her past, she was vivacious, but then a cloud would pass over and appear to steal the joy right out of her soul.

Sensing how difficult this was going to be for her, Rommey softened his voice and took her elbow. She flinched at his touch and stopped cold. He instinctively let go immediately. She gave him a tight-lipped smile and followed him to his office.

"I'm sorry," he said.

"Can we leave the door open?" she asked.

"Um, sure," he said. He wanted to lock the outer door to make sure they weren't interrupted but sensed that

106

would be uncomfortable for her, so he left it unlocked and hoped for privacy.

"After carefully reading the parchment and lamenting again about not knowing him afterward, she signed and resigned herself to the process.

"Are you comfortable? Still want to continue?"

"Yes, on both accounts. Let's get it done," she said.

"Okay, first I need a good memory from your past, or you can pledge a memory from the future."

"I'm not about to give up anything good in my future. My future is all I have. I'm leaving all the past with you. Let's see, the only thing good I remember from my childhood is swinging on the tire swing in my back yard. It was a lonely childhood, but somehow flying weightlessly on that swing made me feel like a could soar away from there to anywhere I could imagine."

Rommey thought it was heartbreaking, but said only, "Okay, why don't you tell me what's bothering you."

"Do I start at the beginning?"

"That usually works best," he replied

"What if I'm not sure when it started? I was very young. I'm…it's kinda fuzzy."

Oh no, don't let it be what I think it is. Let it be petty jealousy of something. Anything but that. Anything but that horror. Rommey begged the cosmos. "Just tell me what you remember."

"I just remember feeling bad and scared whenever my mom's boyfriend was around. Sometimes he'd be super nice and bring me candy or little presents. But then he'd start drinking. I still hate the smell of whiskey. Makes me want to vomit." Her voice had taken on a faraway lilt as if she was just watching from afar, across the ages.

"I'm so sorry." He found himself recoiling in anticipation of the story he knew was coming.

"He'd start calling my name. 'Missy! Missy! Come in here! Daddy wants to see his girl.' I wanted to scream that he was not my daddy, but I didn't dare. When I wouldn't come to him, he'd fly into a rage and I would hide. I'd cram myself into the tiniest spaces, like in the corner under my bed, or in the back of the closet, hoping he wouldn't think to look there. I tried not to eat too much so I could stay small and fit in even tinier spaces, spaces he couldn't reach into. But it usually didn't work. He'd catch me and then tell me I knew I had to be punished for not coming when he called me. He'd take off his belt and tell me to drop my drawers."

Rommey wished he didn't have to hear the rest of Anna's story. Her words turned to anguish, pouring out with strangled grief and horror. Vile greenish-gray abuse mist swirled with the black vapor of horror. It poured from her scalp in torrents. Rommey wondered if the vessel would hold it all.

She described his twisted, straining face, veins standing out on his neck as his body abused her tiny one for its own sick gratification until she could claw her way out as he collapsed in a drunken, satisfied stupor.

"My mom would never be around, of course, when this went on. I still can't face the question of whether she conveniently disappeared or whether he just waited until she was gone. But she had to know. She had to! How could she let him hurt me like that?!" There was a flood of justifiable sobbing for, not only her pain and desecration but also for the betrayal by the person whose allegiance should never have to be questioned.

Rommey handed Anna more tissues as she cried out the last of her vile past and the mist continued to pour into the jug.

"That's why I changed my name as soon as I was old enough. I never wanted to hear anyone call me Missy again. The sound of it makes my blood run cold." She let out a long, shaky breath.

"Are you okay, Anna?"

"I think so. At least, I hope I will be."

"Is there anything else?" Rommey asked.

"Just my whole damned childhood. The best thing that happened to me was Daryl dying in a wreck. Drunk, of course. Naturally, he took my mom with him. I didn't have much but he took everything from me. He was the ruination of everything he touched." She sniffed and wiped her nose again.

"Good riddance," Rommy mumbled.

"Then I went to live with my grandma. Things were peaceful after that. But of course, it was never discussed. I rarely was allowed to ask Grandma about my mother. I don't know if she knew everything or not, but she sure never talked about my life before the wreck. I never really mourned. I just had to pretend nothing happened.

"As I grew up, I just tried to stay out of everyone's sight and not attract attention. Especially from boys. I find dressing like a guy pretty much keeps them from bothering me. But I've been thinking I might like to have a more normal life. Like a girl's life. Maybe meet a nice guy. But I don't think I can do that unless you help me." Anna was sounding very tired as her story came to a close.

"We're almost done, Anna. Why don't you take a little rest."

"I just need to rest my eyes for a few minutes," she slurred a little as she was already drifting off."

He took extra time preparing her tea, adding extra honey to extract every last wisp of her terror, but also just for the sweetness of it. Anna should have a life filled with nothing but sweetness from here on. He added cookies left from his lunch and joined her back in his office.

"Anna, would you like some tea?"

She struggled to open her eyes slightly. "Thank you. How did you know I was so thirsty?" she mumbled.

"Lucky guess." She must have cried a quart of tears.

~~~~~~

After Anna had placed her baseball cap back on her head and quietly closed the door behind her, Rommey stood in the center of his office. He was drained by sharing her trauma. He remembered the vivacious slip of a girl who had somehow managed to brighten the world around her while carrying a traincar load of horror in her young mind. Suddenly, he felt bile rising in his throat. He turned and ran to the toilet where he vomited profusely.

Chapter Twenty

Terrance, Max, and Lavomer

The coffee shop was buzzing with pre-lunch activity when Rommey slipped down there to pick up a tuna sandwich for himself and Reddy to share. He couldn't help but overhear an obnoxiously loud voice over the background sounds of clinking dishes, orders being taken, and names being called out when orders were ready.

There was Terrance with a panicked looking companion as he related example after example of how he had been cheated in life.

"My father was rarely around, and when he was, he wasn't paying me no notice. My mom was working all the time just to keep us fed, so she didn't have time for me neither. I can't never catch no break, you see. The world is against me," he mourned.

The trapped customer checked his watch for the third time in as many minutes and said, "Gee, um that's rough, buddy. I hope things turn around for you. I gotta get back to work. See ya around."

Begrudgingly, Terrance bid him goodbye and cast his eyes around the shop for his next victim. Rommey turned his back to Terrance and tried to keep his head down. He knew he wouldn't be recognized, but he didn't want to be sucked into the audience of Terrance's one-man self-pity opera.

There's always an excuse if you want one, Rommey thought. *Terrance's problem is lethargy, not a bum shoulder or a tough home life. That clip was a waste of my time and a perfectly good cup of tea.*

Rommey was still shaking his head over Terrance as the left the shop. On the patio, there was a young man hunched over a pile of books. Something about him caught Rommey's attention. On a closer look, he realized it was Max, the would-be architect, pouring over a textbook.

Rommey couldn't resist checking on Max, even though Max wouldn't remember him. "Hi. Sorry to bother you. I see you are studying," Rommey said as he approached his table.

Looking up from his work, Max focused for a moment before saying, "Yeah, that's right. Trying to cram in as much as I can before I have to go to work later."

"Good for you. Looks like you are a serious student. What are you studying?" Rommey couldn't keep himself from prying a little to see how Max was doing.

"Architecture. Well, this class is about the history of art and architecture. Fascinating stuff, but there's a lot to know. This section is about the Romanesque period, but then you didn't ask me about all of that, did you? I have a habit of wanting to talk about it endlessly." Max laughed at himself.

"I think it's great. Not everyone takes seriously their chance for education."

"So I've experienced," Max said with a wry smile. "This is my second attempt. I'm working nights waiting tables and taking two classes during the day. Thought I'd get some sunlight for a little while before I get rickets or scurvy or whichever disease is from not seeing the sun for a long time," he laughed.

"It's rickets," Rommey confirmed. "Second attempt, eh? I bet your parents are happy with your decision to go back to school."

"I haven't told them," said Max.

"No? Why not? Don't you think they'll be happy to hear you've gone back?"

"I need to do this by myself, for myself, this time. I want to make my way with money that I earned. Plus, I have to make sure I can do it. I can't bear disappointing them again. This way, it's all on me. I only have myself to depend on. There is only me to let down or please. If I manage my school and workload well, I can take the news to my family without any worry about whether I'll be able to keep it up. If I don't make it, they don't have to be upset again."

"I understand that. Very mature approach. I'll let you get back to it." Rommey shook Max's hand and told him goodbye. "I wish you great success."

"Thanks, man. Nice talking to you." Max bowed his head over his book and went back to his studies.

You win some, you lose some. And sometimes you win by losing. That's one clip I'm glad I lost. Rommey's step was lightened considerably as he made his way back to the office for lunch with Reddy.

~~~~~~

Rommey was just digging back into a manuscript after lunch when he heard the outdoor door open. Lavomer entered the inner office with a flourish.

"Hello, young Rommey," he called. "How art thou?"

"Lavomer, do come in. It's been a while." Rommey walked into the reception area to meet him.

"And you've been busy. You are getting quite close to fulfilling your quota as an Editor." Lavomer let the idea hang in the air.

"Yes, not many clips to go now," Rommey confirmed.

"There are a lot of changes coming up for you," Lavomer flipped the tails of his jacket out of the way and perched on the edge of one of the new chairs Anna had brought.

"I haven't thought them all through, I confess." Rommey put his reading glasses in his shirt pocket and took a seat on the other chair.

"Well, don't wait too long. You'll find yourself jobless before long," Lavomer warned.

"Yes, I know that once my commitment is done, I'll have to create a whole new life for myself. It's exciting, but rather daunting, truthfully." He paused to consider the implications. "Speaking of life after editing, there a particular situation I want to discuss with you."

"That's what I'm here for, to give you guidance."

"There's a girl…"

"Uh oh. Here we go," Lavomer sighed.

"I edited her a while back."

At this, Lavomer visibly cringed. "Don't tell me you're interested in her."

"Well, yeah. I mean, maybe. There's something about her. She brought me these chairs, in fact."

Lavomer looked down, noticing them for the first time. "Nice. I thought something was different. It does look less après rummage sale now, I'll say that."

"See that's what I mean. She seems to brighten everything around her."

"Highly irregular, Rommey. Highly irregular."

"I figured."

"You have an unfair advantage over her. You know the worst that has happened to her. She's completely vulnerable."

"That's why I want to protect her. To make sure no one ever hurts her again."

"There more to a relationship than being someone's superhero."

"I think she could understand my pain – not the whole story, of course. No one could understand my opportunity to earn my life back—I don't understand it myself, frankly. But I think there's an empathy there. Maybe anyway. I'd like to get to know her better and see where it takes us."

Lavomer was frowning during Rommey's plea and he appeared wholly unconvinced. You know she can't remember her pain now, right? You fixed that yourself, if you recall. She's a changed person."

"Yeah, I know. Maybe I'm wrong. I don't even know her. You're right," Rommey admitted dismally.

"Look, I'll leave it to you. Just remember I'm not in favor of it. If you proceed, tread lightly and don't get your hopes up. Her empathy may have just evaporated with her pain. Did you think of that?"

"I hear you, Lavomer. I'll give it more thought."

Chapter Twenty-One

Edward

In the mid-afternoon, there must have been a thug reunion down in the mafia guy's office. There were loud voices, but Rommey couldn't determine whether it was cheering or arguing. Not wanting to be in the area if there was a 'change of management' taking place among the good fellas, he and Reddy padded down to the coffee shop for some air and a change of scenery.

The atmosphere there was much more relaxed than during the morning crush. Reddy claimed a tabled on the patio and waited for Rommey to return with lemon cake, coffee, and a saucer of half and half.

Upon his return, Rommey said, "Nice choice of tables, buddy – just enough sun for you and a little shade for me. Reddy waited expectantly for his corner of cake then lapped up his milk before getting down to the serious business of washing his entire body. Rommey took a seat with his back to the exit door and enjoyed the spring weather as people entered the shop from the other side.

An attractive woman at a nearby table was typing furiously and with great concentration. Mumbling to herself and cursing softly when her apparently balky computer froze up again. Rommey closed his eyes and let the world float away for a bit. There was much to consider for his new life. *Do I want to move? What kind of work will I do? Do I want to keep editing for writers?*

While Rommey daydreamed, the remaining empty table behind Rommey and Reddy was soon claimed by a man with a coffee and a newspaper. Eventually, a nearby conversation wormed into Rommey's brain. He thought he recognized the voice of the man behind him, so he listened a bit longer before turning slightly to steal a glance. Just as he thought, it was Edward Widdlefish, the man who wanted to forget his high school crush.

Edward was in rapt conversation with the cursing typist about their mutual love of red wine and the Atlanta United soccer team.

"Hey, how about I take you to this great restaurant I've found. They have a killer wine list," Rommey overheard Edward say.

"That sounds fun," said the typist.

"How about Saturday?"

"I'd love to. I can meet you there. It's my 'first date rule', or actually my 'first several dates rule'. I always drive myself. You can't be too careful," she explained.

"I completely understand. Can I get your number so I can confirm the time when I get a reservation?" Edward asked.

"Here's my card. That's my cell," she said.

"Great, I'll give you a call when it's all arranged." Edward couldn't stop smiling as he looked at her.

"I gotta run," she said, "but I'm definitely looking forward to dinner. Bye for now." She gave a little wave as she gathered her papers and computer and rushed off.

Well, look at Edward asking out a girl. Without Emmalee to distract him, he's able to function like a normal guy. Rommey was feeling satisfied in his ability to make some lives better, even if it was over a minor issue.

117

As Edward took back his seat, the smile drained from his face. He looked down at the typist's card on the table. He read it, then flipped it over to see if there was more information there. Finding none, he shrugged, dropped the card into his empty cup, and threw away his trash, including the card.

As Edward rose to leave, he walked past Rommey. "Hey man, sounds like you got yourself a date with that woman. She seems very nice," Rommey offered.

Edward cocked his head in puzzlement and said, "What woman?"

"The one you were talking to. Sorry, I couldn't help but overhear."

"Man, I don't know what you're talking about," Edward said as he strode away.

Rommey was puzzled but then understood. Edward's future good memory pledge was now paid in full.

Chapter Twenty-Two

Mark

"So, Mark, you've been here for a while now, healing, thinking, resting. Have you decided if you want to redeem your life by becoming an Editor as we discussed?" asked Lavomer.

"I've been giving it a lot of thought since the option was offered to me..." Mark paused.

"And?"

"I think about going back there and the pain the world still holds. None of that has changed. Here in purgatory, or whatever you call this place..."

"Between."

"Between what?"

"This place. It's called Between," said Lavomer.

"Let's just say there is a lot of time to think here in Between."

"Precisely. That is its main purpose. However, your time to decide is coming to an end. You must go back as an Editor or continue on."

"To where? What is the 'continue on' option?" asked Mark.

"I can't tell you that," said Lavomer.

"Why not? It's my life we're talking about here." Frustration was rising in his voice.

"First of all, it's not 'your life'. You ended that if you will recall. Second, I can't tell you what happens if you 'continue on' because I don't know. This is my station. I've never been farther, nor have I met anyone who has," answered Lavomer.

"Oh," Mark said quietly," retracting his misplaced indignation.

"If you want to regain a semblance of the life you threw away, causing several people a great deal of heartache, including a very sweet lady named Evelyn who tried to help you by the way…" Lavomer stopped here to catch his breath and to calm his rising level of irritation with Mark. "You have one chance to do that. If not, your spot will go to someone else in Between."

"I'm not as ready to leave my earthly life as I thought. I've had enough time to work through some of the hopelessness and pain I felt."

"I'm glad to hear that. If you choose to edit, you will learn from your clients what one can overcome, and when to ask for help. Plus, helping others can be therapeutic in itself. You'll see."

"You sound like I've already decided to say 'yes' to editing," said Mark.

"I think you have, but I need to hear you say it," said Lavomer.

"Okay," Mark exhaled unsteadily. "Make me an Editor."

"Excellent." Lavomer clasped his hands together. "The current Editor in our sector will soon finish his assignment."

"Whew, so here I go." The task ahead of him was just starting to become real. "So how does it work? I have so many questions." Mark said.

"First, when we are ready for you, your body will be repaired and precipitated back to tangible form. You'll be provided with an office where your clients will be directed once you are settled. I suggest you get an apartment nearby since you'll have no money for a car for some time. The lifestyle is meager, but you'll survive. Ha, survive, did you catch that? Oh, and when a stray dog or cat shows up, take it in. You're going to need it. You can get pretty lonely when everyone you meet forgets you," finished Lavomer.

"What? Why would they forget me?"

"I'll explain as we prepare you for the job."

Mark was still looking troubled as more and more questions came to him. "You said I'd be an editor as well as an Editor?"

"That's right."

"How do I know how to edit books? I was never that good in English, truthfully."

"It's all part of the service we provide. Kind of a package deal, if you will. That skill will be added to your memory when you are reconstituted as if you've known it all your life," said Lavomer.

"This is a lot to take in." Mark was looking a bit overwhelmed.

"You'll get the hang of it. I have every confidence in you. It's as easy as jumping off a bridge!" Laughter burst from Lavomer. "See what I did there? I'm on a roll tonight!"

"Too soon, man. Too soon." Mark chuckled despite resisting.

"Sorry, gallows humor. It's an unfortunate consequence of the trade. Oh, and you'll need a new name."

"Why? Oh yeah, Mark Fallon is dead."

"Right. Your Editor name doesn't have to be permanent. You can change to something else once your commitment is complete. For your Editor name, you can select what you like, but historically, it is a play on what we do," counseled Lavomer. "For example, Lavomer L. Lacer is recaLL removaL backward. See? Clever, eh? I was thinking Amin Rotide for you, but if you don't like that or have a better idea, that's fine."

Mark tried to work out the word puzzle in his head but came out empty. "Amin Rotide?"

"Scramble the letters and you have 'I'm an Editor'," Lavomer said with a grin.

"Amin Rotide. Amin," Mark tried it on for size. "'Hey Amin, how's it going?', 'Nice to meet you, Amin.'" Satisfied, Mark said, "Yeah, that works. When do I start?" The idea was growing on him.

"I'll be by to get you in a short period of time. It will be a taxing but exciting time so get some rest," Lavomer said.

"That's all I've been doing for a very long time," Mark smiled and felt excitement for this new challenge beginning to build. "Thanks, Lavomer. I'm glad to be moving on and to have something to look forward to."

Lavomer tipped his hat and vanished.

Chapter Twenty-Three

Jacob

The time finally came when Jacob walked through Rommey's door with a white card in this hand. He was looking at the vaulted ceiling and commanding view when Rommey appeared out of his office. Rommey's heart sank when he saw him, knowing that soon one of the few people he had talked with on a non-business basis would not remember him.

"Hi, Jacob."

Jacob whirled around and looked at Rommey with a puzzled expression. "Your last name is Clipper?"

"Yep."

"Then this is your card."

"It appears to be," said Rommey calmly. Reddy jumped down and wound himself around Jacob's legs.

"Hey, Reddy! How's the man? I should have made the connection between you and the card. I've never met anyone else named Rommey. So, did you slip the card into my pocket when we met in the bar?"

"No."

"Then how did...when...why am I here? In your office, I mean, not on here on earth. I'm just...can I sit down for a minute?"

Rommey showed him to the seating area. Jacob lowered himself onto one of Anna's chairs.

I'll always think of them as Anna's chairs. He gave Jacob a minute to collect himself. *Changeable Anna. I hope the light within her is brightening the world around her now. Her entire childhood was a train wreck, but at least the most horrible part is gone now. Live your best life, Anna.* He sent his wish for her into the cosmos before returning his attention to Jacob.

"You might want to put your head between your knees. People find it helps with the dizziness," Rommey advised.

"You've seen this before?"

"Happens all the time. Can I get you some water or something?"

Jacob looked up at Rommey, who was still standing. "Tell me how you got the card inside my house…on my nightstand."

"I didn't do that," said Rommey.

"How then? I don't remember you ever giving me your card."

"That's right."

"And the dreams? And me thinking I see your name everywhere?" asked Jacob.

"I honestly don't know how that works. I just know if a person needs help with plaguing memories, they hear or see or read messages, and often wind up in my office."

"But why?"

"Because I can help them. If they want, that is," said Rommey.

"And you do what? Hypnotize them or something?"

"No, I edit their memory."

Jacob looked more confused than ever as Rommey explained the basics. After hearing about the process and outcome, Jacob said, "What if the person with the bad memory is the reason for it? I mean, what if he is not the victim, but the perpetrator?"

"I've helped several people who made mistakes or bad choices. They are not evil people. They deserved to be freed from the burden of the memory at some point. None of us goes through life without our share of misguided choices."

Jacob thought for several minutes before confiding quietly, "But what I did was bad. Horrible, stupid, arrogant, and unforgivable."

"Was it on purpose?" Rommey asked.

"Well, no, but I should have known better. I was young. I thought we were bulletproof, you know?"

"Yeah, I do. Better than you might think."

"I'm so haunted by it. Maybe I'm not entitled to forget. Maybe my punishment is to always remember until I die," lamented Jacob.

"Only you can decide that."

"If that's my punishment, I don't think I can bear it any longer. Everyone said it was an accident. Even my buddy Dallas' parents said they forgave me, but I can't accept that. He's gone forever. It should have been me. I was driving…"

Rommey chest tightened. It was hard to catch his breath. "I need you to stop there, Jacob." *This is too much. Too familiar. How can I listen to this story from someone else?*

Jacob was startled and looked up with tears brimming in his eyes.

Scrambling to regain his composure, Rommey stalled Jacob. "You can't tell me what happened unless you are sure you want me to subtract it from your memories. In fact, you might want to go and think about it for a while. I mean, now that you know what your options are here." Rommey concealed his shaking hands in his pockets.

"You think?" asked Jacob.

"It's up to you," Rommey said, trying to do the right thing and leave the decision to Jacob.

"I don't know. I do know I can't continue to carry this around. The shame, the remorse. It sits on my chest like a physical being, making it hard to breathe or to think about anything else."

"I know."

"You do?"

"I mean, I can imagine," said Rommey.

"So, you could make it so I could forget the whole incident?"

"I can. It's truly up to you."

"Would that be right? I mean, morally?" asked Jacob.

"I can't answer that."

"His parents forgave me. They said they didn't want the incident to ruin my life, too."

"Kind people," said Rommey.

"And there is no good coming of the memory," Jacob added. His lips were pressed tight as he considered his options. Rommey waited silently. After a long sigh, Jacob said, "I want to do it. Frankly, it's this or …I can't take the guilt and despair anymore."

"I know one thing for sure," said Rommey.

"What's that?"

"Suicide is not the answer."

Jacob looked down, gathering his resolve.
"Sometimes it seems like the only way to the end the hell I'm living in."

"It's not. I can help you." As Rommey turned toward his office, motioning for Jacob to follow him, he gritted his teeth and steeled himself for the story he knew was coming—a story he knew too well. It was a retelling that would rip his wounds open as it healed Jacob's. But he had to do it to save Jacob and give him peace. It was his duty.

"Have you decided whether to give up an old memory or a future one?" Rommey asked.

"I'd rather give up a future one, but I guess I'd better give up my memories of Dallas. Otherwise, when I think of him, I might wonder what happened to him. I wouldn't do for me to go looking for him, would it?"

"It definitely would not."

"But to forget all the fun we had together all the friendship. I can't just dump that in the trash." Jacob's eyes filled with tears.

"True. That would leave a big hole in your childhood. And maybe even change the kind of person you grew up to be. Hmm." Rommey paused to think. "How about if you give me one memory, then I can remind you that he passed away so you don't go searching for him?"

"That might work. I really want to remember him and how much he meant to me."

"Done. Now, what memory will you give up?

Jacob thought for a moment, then said, "The year he gave me a super-soaker for my birthday, just like the one he had gotten for his. I don't think we were ever dry that entire summer." Jacob smiled at the remembrance.

"Got it. Okay just relax and tell me your memories," coached Rommey as he set up the receiving vessel.

Jacob told Rommey about Dallas and how they'd been best friends since middle school had thrown them together alphabetically. "Everyone called him 'Dallas' because he would not shut up about the Cowboys. We played soccer together, mostly warming the bench. Over the years we struggled through geometry, wondered about girls, and unfortunately one night, we got drunk together." It wasn't an original story, but it was no less tragic when a night of intoxicated driving turned into hospitalization for one and a funeral for the other. Jacob's anguished tears halted his recollections for a moment.

At this point, Rommey felt the bile rise in his throat, threatening to interrupt the session. It was all he could do to keep from crying with Jacob as the black mist of fear and terror swirled with the white of sorrow and the brown of regret which spooled away from Jacob as he sobbed.

When he was sure Jacob was finished, Rommey rose, laid a hand on his shoulder, and told him to rest. He capped the jug as he headed to the kitchen, thinking his own memory would look very much like this ugly mixture of heartbreak.

Rommey absently stirred the tea while his mind reeled with the gut-wrenching memories of a wreck with a similar outcome. Like Jacob, though his physical body healed, Rommey's mind would not forget, would not forgive him for his errors behind the wheel. It would not stop asking "what if" I had made other choices or had been more cautious. It would not release him from the guilt and the sickening pain. So, he had found a way to stop it—to stop it all for good. He knew now that suicide was the wrong choice, but at the time it seemed like the only way to stop the soul grinding despair.

Rommey realized he was stirring Jacob's tea without remembering making it. He poured a cup for himself to soothe his pounding head and went to wake his weary friend. He roused Jacob and handed him the tea while suggesting that he never drink and drive and that he cherish his loved ones every day. He also reminded him that Dallas had passed away, as promised. This news brought on silent tears that quickly resolved to acceptance. Once Jacob had recovered a bit, Rommey escorted him to the door.

By his act, Rommey had given a tortured man a chance to live in peace, but he had also assured the fact that his friend - a scarcity in his life - would not remember ever having met him. It was with the pull of sadness in his chest that he watched Jacob walk dreamily out of his life.

Then something occurred to him. Checking his appointment book, he verified that Jacob was his thirtieth edit. He was finished. He would have his life back, and his memories if he wanted them. Or he could replace his history with the good remembrances sacrificed by others and modified into a realistic lifetime by The Editorial Council who performed that service. It would be his option. His heart pounded in this chest, but this time it was not from the pain of his and Jacob's tragic stories, but the promise of a second chance he had worked so long to earn.

When Lavomer came calling, Rommey knew what his choice would be.

Chapter Twenty-Four

Rommey

The morning after Jacob's edit, Rommey sat in one of Anna's chair with Reddy in his lap. He gazed across the city, absently stroking the cat, and wondered what would happen next. *Am I just supposed to vacate the office so the next editor can move in? What if someone comes to be edited before he or she arrives? I can't just turn them away. Some people are in grave need, at the end of their ability to cope when they come to me. No, I'll stay on duty until Lavomer or someone comes for me. I have several manuscripts waiting for me, so I can easily stay busy.*

Does Lavomer know I'm finished? I wish there was a way to contact him. Did I count the clips correctly? He began running through the list again in his mind when there was a light knock at the door. Lavomer and Mark Fallon, now Amin Rotide, walked into his office. Mark was still a little rocky on his feet as he worked to get the hang of having a corporeal body again.

"Good morning, Rommey. I'd like for you to meet Amin Rotide, your replacement."

There was an unexpected tug of loss for the job he knew he was leaving, the job that had taught him so much, and earned him a second chance at life. He extended his hand and said with a half-smile, "Welcome Amin."

"Nice to meet you, Rommey."

"Now Rommey, you have some decisions to make. Hopefully, you've already made them. First, are you sticking with Rommey Clipper?" Lavomer turned to Amin and said, "His name was not *that* clever. Rommey is just the rearrangement of the letters in 'memory'. So, he is Memory Clipper." Amin nodded his understanding.

"I've decided to stick with Rommey. I've gotten used to it. Besides, I'd like to think that guy helped a lot of people. You know, Lavomer, I always thought your name sounded like a guy from some eastern bloc country. Maybe Transylvania or something. Very old world. Mysterious." Rommey made a *whooo* spooky sound and held his hands up as if he was casting a spell.

Amin smiled at the banter between the two old friends, and his shoulders begin to relax a little.

"Very funny. Yes, I chose something a little more *this century* for my new name when I finished my commitment."

"And what did you choose for your post-Editor name?" Rommey asked.

"None of your business," Lavomer sniffed.

Rommey chuckled. Lavomer chose to be elusive about the strangest things. Rommey never saw it coming. He shook his head and continued, "But Lavomer L Lacer – Recall Removal, was inspired, I'll give you that. And for my cat, Redactor, I'll just keep calling him Reddy. It suits my orange boy, I think." He turned to Amin, "So are you ready to meet your first client? Do you know what to do?"

"I've been practicing," Amin smiled sheepishly.

"Oh, the tea and honey supplies are running low," said Rommey.

"Chamomile, right?" asked Amin.

"You got it. You're going to be fine. It's pretty routine once you've been through it a few times. They'll send you some easier cases at first."

Amin was looking calmer as the conversation wore on.

Then Rommey was serious for a moment, "Some of these people will break your heart, or make your head pound with fury over the wrongs they have endured. Your job is to stay strong for them so they can get it all out. It won't always be easy, but it is worthwhile. And it will help you to continue to heal as well. I'm living proof." Rommey burst out laughing then. "Living proof! Get it? Living?" There was laughter all around.

"And what about your memories, Rommey? Are you going to keep yours or trade them in on a less painful collection?" asked Lavomer.

"No question. I'm keeping my own. I think the person we are is the product of our experiences and how we deal with those memories. I don't want to forget my brother. Our parents are gone now, so memories of them are all I have. I don't even have pictures or keepsakes since I was, um *gone,* for a while. I'll keep my memories."

"As you wish," said Lavomer. "You may now re-enter the world on your own terms. Do you think you will keep editing books and such?"

"I do. Someone has to. There are comma splices and dangling participles to be slain. I'll be saving the world from misplaced modifiers, one manuscript at a time. And, truly, there are some gifted writers out there with stories to tell. I'd like to continue to be part of that." Sargent Gipson came to mind. Rommey was looking forward to continuing to work with him on the memoir and giving his incredible story its very best shot.

He made a mental note to send emails to his writer clients to only contact him by email until he got a new office set up. He might even get a phone for the convenience of his clients.

Amin found his voice at last. "Rommey, can you tell me how you got here? I mean, if it's not too personal or painful. I'm feeling pretty shaky about my ability to do what needs to be done here. I mean, who am I to help others when I didn't help myself? Maybe if I hear your story, I'll have a better perspective or a little more confidence."

Rommey took a deep breath and closed his eyes for a moment. *If I'm going to keep this memory for the rest of my life, I must learn to live with it, to own it. Here goes.*

Lavomer knew the story, but Rommey told Amin how he and his brother had gone to the concert for Jamie's birthday. "We both drank at the concert. Afterward, we were a little buzzed but mostly exhausted. I fell asleep behind the wheel regained consciousness in a world of flashing lights and rescue personnel at the scene of their wreck."

"My name was David, then. I woke up again in the hospital still confused and looking for Jamie, but no one would tell me anything. When they finally did, I wished they hadn't. If they hadn't told me, I could have kept hoping, assuming, praying that Jamie was okay. But of course, he wasn't."

Rommey took a heavy breath before continuing. "The next weeks were a fog of headaches and painkillers. They had to keep telling me Jamie had died because I couldn't remember any of it. Ironic, huh, since later all I wanted to do was forget? Anyway, every time someone would tell me, it was like hearing it for the first time. The anguish of that horrible, unbelievable, unfathomable news broke across me over and over, knocking me like a tidal wave. I didn't even get to say 'goodbye'. I never saw him again because I was in the hospital with a serious head injury and

several broken bones while they buried my brother."
Rommey stopped to clear his throat so he could speak
again. "Little Jamie. He was my responsibility and I killed
him." Rommey broke down and gritted out, "I killed my
brother. Oh god, Jamie. I'm sorry. I miss you. Every
fucking day, I miss you!" Rommey sprung out the chair in
fury and walked into his office.

Amin's eyes were large as he wordlessly asked
Lavomer if they should do something. Lavomer raised his
hand to tell Amin to just give Rommey a minute to
compose himself.

After blowing his nose and splashing some water on
his face, Rommey returned to the reception area where
Amin and Lavomer were waiting silently.

"I'm sorry man, I didn't mean to…" started Amin.

But Rommey cut Amin off. "It's a story I have to own.
I needed to get it out." He took his chair and a deep breath
and continued. "There was counseling for grief and for
guilt. There were my friends Jack, Jim, and Johnny Walker
to keep me company at the bottom of a glass at every bar
around. They could dull the pain and guilt for an hour or
so, but even while drunk, it's not like I could forget. Like
the card says, 'To forgive is difficult. To forget is
impossible.' I couldn't forgive myself for the unforgivable.
I certainly couldn't forget it. Only if I passed out, was I
free. When I sobered up, I'd feel guilty for trying to escape
like a coward.

"I wasn't strong enough to carry the weight of the
remorse. In my defense, how could anyone forgive
themselves? I'd never forgive someone else for killing
Jamie, so how could I possibly forgive myself? And I
loved him more than anyone. I was the one who was
supposed to protect him, to watch out after him. But,
then…" He paused again to compose himself.

"The sadness and self-loathing built up to a point that I knew I could never be free of it. It would never stop. Never lessen. No one could help me with that. I thought I didn't deserve to be helped. I just couldn't bear to keep living. A handful of tranquilizers plus all the booze I could drink before I passed out did the trick. I didn't wake up, at least, not until I reached Between. Well, you know what Between is like, so here we both are, Amin. Like you, Between is where I finally learned not how to leave it all behind, but how to manage it. Being given the chance to live again, and to help others...well, obviously, you've made the same choice I did.

"To misquote Malvolio and Mr. Shakespeare, 'Some people are born to tragedy, some create tragedy, and some have tragedy thrust upon them.' You'll see all of those circumstances in the work ahead of you. I wish you great success. Don't lose yourself in the tragedy of others."

"Good advice," said Amin. "I appreciate it."

"No charge, man. Good luck." With that, Rommey was a free man.

Chapter Twenty-Five

Anna

Now that Rommey was free from his daily duties as The Editor, he looked forward to starting a new normal life with friends and people he could talk to more than a time or two. He had kept his apartment and was working from there on his laptop until he could find an affordable office for his fledgling editing business.

He and Reddy headed to the park to soak in the spring sunlight. It poured through chartreuse leaves which gave a lively green glow to the whole place. A girl walked by while reading a book, somehow managing to step over a paper cup on the walkway without looking at it. *It's like she had a sixth sense or an understanding... or something.*

A memory jolted Rommey like an electric shock. "*An understanding...or something.*" He had heard that exact phrase before. *Could it be? Could it be Anna, the girl who dressed like a boy to avoid attention from men?* Her hair was longer now and in a sleek bob. She wore no makeup, but she didn't need any. And she was dressed in a pretty floral blouse and women's jeans. Her phrase, 'like a girl', came back to him in her voice from so many months ago. She looked different, but it was definitely her. Her posture was more relaxed, more natural now. She didn't cower to try to be invisible. When he saw the clover-shaped birthmark near her wrist, he was positive. He remembered seeing it when she was moving the chairs into position at his office. It was definitely Anna. Intelligent, intriguing Anna.

The lightness of the spring air and his newfound freedom gave him the courage to approach her.

"Hi, I couldn't help but notice your book."

"You've read *Watership Down*? Cute cat. I'm Anna."

"Yes. That's Reddy, and I'm Rommey."

"Hey, Reddy! Handsome boy. Did you know almost all orange cats are male?

"No, I didn't." They turned in an unspoken agreement to head down the path together. It all felt so natural, Rommey didn't even notice the synchronized movement.

"Yeah, It's a sex-linked gene."

"Please, tell me more about that," urged Rommey.

"Really? Most people hear a bit of science and turn away. I just think it is fascinating and can't wait to share the info. However, not everyone appreciates that, I find," she said, laughing at herself.

"I think it's charming. Are you enjoying *Watership Down*?" he asked.

"I love it. It's a great adventure story, but there is a whole separate level of social commentary. C. S. Lewis is such a clever writer. Supposedly he didn't intend to write an allegory. Maybe that's why it so subtle."

"Maybe he had a good editor," Rommey chuckled.

Anna turned and looked at him quizzically, but let it pass. "Maybe, but right now, I confess, I'm worried about the rabbits being able to get across the creek! Silly, I know, but it is stressing me!"

"I think it's delightful that you are so engrossed in the characters." As they rounded the bend, Rommey said, "Hey look, a playground. How about a swing?"

"Weird, I can't remember ever having swung," she furrowed her brow as she tried to remember. "I bet you'll love it. Come on."

About the Author

———

Donna H. Black writes fiction, non-fiction, and poetry. Construction manager, horticulturist, photographer, and gardener, Donna rejoices in family and nature, and struggles with the rest of the world in middle Georgia.

For information about permission to reproduce any portion of this book, contact the author at:
donnablackwrites@gmail.com

Read and subscribe to her blog for more of her writing and updates on writing projects at:
http://donnablackwrites.wordpress.com

Contact her via Facebook at: donnablackwrites

Other Works by This Author

————————

Rain and Wind: Collected Poems was released in
May of 2020.

Risk Tolerance, a work of adult fiction about a
woman who embarks on construction project that will
take her just far enough away from her marriage and
motherhood to allow her neglected self to reawaken,
jeopardizing all she values, is expected to be released
in 2021.

Made in the USA
Columbia, SC
23 June 2021